Seasons of Us

The Keenan Legacy Series

Marina Alexa

Marina Alexa

CONTENTS

PLAYLIST

1. I Know the End – Phoebe Bridgers

2. Mountain With A View – Kelsea Ballerini

3. Northern Attitude – Noah Kahan

4. Slower – Tate McRae

5. How Do I Do This – Kelsea Ballerini

6. Right Back to It – Wazahatchee

7. Messy – ROSE

8. Heartbroken – Diplo, Jessie Murph & Polo G

9. Call It What You Want – Taylor Swift

10. Starting Over – Chris Stapleton

DEDICATION

For the ones who choose to leave, rebuild, and believe again. These words are for you.

Chapter One

Avery

I drag the brush through my hair, each stroke slower than the last. The mirror stares back at me, daring me to look, but I can't. Most days, I'd twist my hair into a braid or knot it into a tight bun, but tonight it hangs loose, the way my mother always preferred. She used to say it softened my "full" face, her delicate way of pointing out flaws. But, for my mother, that was practically a compliment.

Growing up, our family was the opposite of warm or loving. I could count the times we hugged or said *I love you* on one hand. Despite having four kids in four years, my parents never seemed interested in having a family. They were present—they didn't ditch us for a beach house in Aruba, letting the nanny raise us, even though they could have. They just didn't seem to want to be there. And you would think that our parents' lack of emotional support would make me and my siblings close, but not us Keenans. We were just as emotionally stunted and distant as our parents, which is why, on the morning of our mother's funeral, we weren't together. Instead, we were all separate with the plan to meet at the funeral home and leave immediately after with as little face time together as possible.

I couldn't blame them. We're all screwed up, and now that both of our parents are dead, I don't think any of us knows what it means. Once the will is read and the money is split up, would we ever talk? Would we try to stay a family? I'm the youngest of the four of us and the only one who got married—everyone else is alone, but I seem to be the only one trying to keep us together.

Abigail, the oldest of us, is a high-paying attorney in New York. She is the definition of 'married to their work.' She never dates, not that she would tell me if she did, but who needs a man when you make seven figures a year?

Anthony, the rebel child, is a professional MMA fighter and one of the greatest. He never lets anything faze him and moves like a machine built for the cage. I've never told him this, but I'm convinced he was born for it. I've only seen one of his fights in person, but I watch almost all of them on Pay-Per-View. It's something to witness—raw, controlled, and just a little magical.

Adam, the neurosurgeon in the making, works hundred-hour weeks and insists he has no time for family pleasantries like phone calls. He's sharp, focused, and always juggling something, whether it's his studies, his patients, or the pieces of a life he rarely talks about.

And me, Avery, the youngest of four, and the most-requested high-end event planner on the East Coast. But since I don't have a title with "chief" or "partner" in it, my family likes to call it the "party girl" job.

Even though the four of us are not close, I can't help but wonder how they are feeling. Did they just spend the last hour gazing into a mirror, wondering how the hell we ended up here, or are they just itching to get our mother into the ground and get back to work? I pick up my phone off my bed, reading the latest text that came through moments ago.

> **Campbell:** Running late at work. Will be there when I can.

I roll my eyes. I should be surrounded by family and loved ones today, caring for me and making sure I'm okay. But instead, I have three siblings who want to be anywhere other than here and a husband who can't get away from work for his mother-in-law's funeral. I shake my head as though it will get rid of the anger I feel bubbling up in my body.

I do everything alone. I can do this alone too.

✱✱✱

The funeral home is stuffy and freezing. You wouldn't know it was June in New York based on the temperature here. My short black dress now seems like a big mistake, and I internally scold myself for not choosing the black slacks and collared shirt I first tried on this morning. Sleeves and pants sound like a great option now.

The place is swarming with old colleagues and ac-
quaintances of my parents, here out of some distorted
sense of obligation. The truth is, my parents didn't have
friends—they had people who made their lives match the
pretty picture they painted for the world to see.

It's suffocating. Every handshake, every strained smile
feels rehearsed, like everyone is playing a role they've
been cast in for years. I'm not even sure if anyone here
actually liked my parents, but it doesn't seem to matter.
They're here to pay their respects, to keep up appear-
ances, to be seen doing the "right" thing. And I, like everyone else, am expected to do the same—hold my head
high, say all the right things, and play my part perfectly.

I look down at my phone, frowning at the lack of an
update from Campbell. We've been married for almost a
year, and it's been...content... He comes from the same
family circle of friends, and it was written when we were
still in the womb that we were to be married. I honestly can't say anything bad about him, but our relationship is...lackluster. No passion, no feelings, a business
arrangement like every other part of my life, which gen-
erally would be fine, except part of our arrangement is
that we show up. We'd show up at the work parties and
the silly engagements we were expected to appear at,
even though we'd prefer to be anywhere else.

We show up. Except, he's not here. My mother's funeral is going to start in fifteen minutes, and he's not here.
I tighten my fists, feeling my nails dig into my palm, the
anger bubbling again, but I see Anthony stumble through
the door before it can boil over. He looks disheveled, his

black tie is lopsided and loose as he tries to get the other arm of his suit jacket on as he walks toward me. As soon as he's within arm's reach, I smell the whiskey protruding from his pores.

"Anthony," I scold. "Could you not shower?"

As I look closer, I spot the dark circles under his eyes, like he hasn't slept in days. I want to ask him if he's okay. If he hasn't slept because of our mother, they always had a bond. I remember that, as a kid, I would see her watching him from the kitchen window playing football, and anytime he would fall or take a tackle, she would be so worried that she would immediately run and make sure he was okay. He was the only one she showed that motherly overprotectiveness—she must've hated when he started to fight for a living.

"Little sister." He gleams. "What is a family reunion without a drunk sibling? I just figured I'd take the reins on this one."

His words reek of a self-deprecating plea for help, and Abigail and Adam appear next to us before I can respond.

"Avery, you look beautiful," Abigail says as she leans toward me, placing a soft kiss on my cheek. Very formal, just like her. I take her in after not seeing her for months. Her long brown hair is down, looking nearly identical to mine as she captures the room in an all-black business suit appropriate for a funeral, and would have no problem walking right out of here and into a courtroom, which is most likely what she has planned. *I bet she's not freezing like me.*

"Thanks, Abigail. You do too." I smile softly. I look to Adam, who is now tightening Anthony's tie. From the outside I bet we look like a real family.

"Are you guys ready?" I sigh, looking at the three of them.

They all nod in agreement. I take a breath and lead us toward the double doors into the main room where everyone else has gathered. The room with the casket holding my mother's dead body. The room I've been try- ing to avoid since I've arrived. It's not the fact that it's a dead body. I didn't have this issue at my father's funeral or my cousin Danielle's when I was a kid, but knowing my mother is in there makes my body spiral into fight or flight. She was such a force growing up. No one wanted to deal with the wrath of Cinzia Keenan. People either loved her or feared her—there was no in-between—and I think she liked it that way.

We find our seats and sit quietly, waiting for the priest to start and say a few words. He goes through a prayer and talks about how she is now in a better place with my father. All words that would be comforting if she believed in God or heaven, but I never once heard her talk about religion growing up. Religion means faith and hope, and that means vulnerability and feelings, which are two things she never had. No, I don't think my mother believed in anything.

I zone out in my thoughts, completely missing the poem my aunt Anna read and the song one of my younger cousins sang. When I finally come out of my trance, Abigail, Anthony, and Adam are all staring at me and waiting.

"What?" I ask, confused.

"One of us needs to say something," Adam says expectantly.

"And?"

"We think it should be you."

"What!" I shout and quickly bow down cowardly.

"You're the youngest." Anthony shrugs.

Ah. The excuse I've been getting since I was old enough to talk. The one that leaves me no rebuttal because it automatically puts me three against one.

"No," I say, staying firm. "I won't do it. One of you needs to step up. What about you, Abs? How about the oldest goes?"

"Avery," she says softly but firm. "Get up right now before we continue to embarrass ourselves."

And that's it. The conversation is over. There's no point in fighting, my fate is already sealed. I sigh, getting up, my hands running over my dress to smooth it out.

"You're going to regret this," I hiss to the three of them as I step toward the podium.

I wipe my clammy hands against my dress, trying to think about what I'll say when I make it up there, but my mind is blank. I stand behind the small wooden podium, adjusting the microphone to match the height of my mouth.

"Hello, everyone," I say, although it comes out more as a whisper. I clear my throat, trying to sum up any confidence I have in my body. "My siblings and I are so grateful for each of you coming here today."

I take a moment to look into the audience. Our extended family is small, so most of the people in this room were colleagues of my father or club members with my mother. I wonder if there is anyone my mother considered a genuine friend who's now sitting out here.

"My mother would have been grateful too," I continue. "If there was one thing Cinzia Kennan appreciated, it was a good show." I laugh and see everyone hold their breath as if they aren't sure where I will go next. I mean, there are two routes I could take, *right?*

The first is the dutiful daughter where I laugh that comment off and go into a short but sweet memory that paints my mother in a good light.

The second is to expose the hypocrisy of this funeral and essentially dance on her grave. Unfortunately, I'm slightly buzzed, my nerves are shot, and my brain decides to choose the latter.

"Give me a show of hands...how many of you were close to my mother? I mean, actually close to her. Did anyone consider her a friend?"

No hands go up, but I think it's maybe because I've shocked everyone into oblivion. I see the slight O to everyone's lips as the words spill from my lips. "In my twenty-eight years of life, I don't think I've seen any of you outside of an office or business function, family excluded. And let's be honest, excluded barely."

Now my eyes find my siblings. Abigail is sneakily looking at her phone—probably not even aware her sister is making an ass out of herself. I give Anthony and Adam credit, they both look like they are ready to jump up and pull me down any second, but are cautiously waiting. I'm sure slightly intrigued about where I take this.

"Let's just call this what it is. This isn't a funeral—this is a charade. One last parade for the Kennans and one last chance for you to suck up to the kids. The kids who are now set to inherit their parents' fortune along with the family business that funds many of *your* businesses, am I right?"

Now Anthony is on his feet, walking toward me, and I figure I might as well go down swinging. I take the microphone off the stand, moving farther away from my brother's footsteps.

"I mean, people, let's be real. The four of us aren't going to take over. We're going to sell it. Liquidate the assets, split the money, and probably never speak to each other or any of you again." My words taste bitter as they come out of my mouth, and I feel tears pool in my eyelids involuntarily. I blink, forcing them away, and turn my body so it's now facing the open casket. It's the first time I've actually looked at her in there. The black dress she loved fits her corpse perfectly, her hair and makeup done to an over-exuberant level, but nice nonetheless. She looks beautiful, at peace.

I take a deep breath before whispering, "A poetic ending to a tragic life."

I drop the microphone and leave, immediately regretting the last five minutes.

CHAPTER TWO

Avery

As soon as I step out of the funeral home, I head to the alley next to the building. My hand flies to my chest as I try to slow down my heart rate. I lean my back against the brick wall, placing my hands on my bare knees in an effort to take deep breaths.

"What the fuck did I just do?" I mutter to myself, still forcing air into my lungs.

"It was epic," I hear Anthony's voice ring in my ears, and I tilt my head to get a look at his face.

"Yeah?" I question, not sure if he's being serious or not.

"Someone might as well tell the truth around here." He shrugs as he leans against the wall beside me.

"My brother, the eternal optimist." Sarcasm is evident in my voice, but I do feel better knowing he's not mad.

He stares at me for a moment longer. "You okay?"

I lean my body up to stand straight. "I'm okay. Thanks."

For a minute, I think he'll come in for a hug, but he stays in his place, and so do I. Moments later, Abigail and Adam are in the alleyway with us.

"Way to show our hand. Now, they know we want to sell," Abigail says, once again staring at her phone.

"Abigail, politely fuck off. You haven't looked up from your phone for more than five minutes this whole day. I just said what we were all thinking." Mimicking what my brother said moments ago.

"Well, Avery, that's the problem, right?" Adam interrupts. "The thinking doesn't get us in trouble, but your little teenage tantrum or whatever you want to define what just happened in there—that does."

I don't like disappointing people. I'm a pathological people pleaser by nature, but the condescension ringing off his words is about to push me over the edge.

"Leave her alone. It's done. Who gives a shit anyhow?"

I sigh, thankful to Anthony for ending the conversation. I drag my hands down my face and shake my hair, which suddenly feels very heavy.

"What do we want to do about the house? What about Mom and Dad's stuff? Should we go there now?" I suggest.

"Uh, no." Abigail is the first to speak up. "I've already been gone from work far too long."

"Yeah, I have surgery in an hour. I need to go."

"Let's just hire people to do it," Abigail suggests.

"Yeah, fine." I wave them off. "See you at whoever's funeral is next."

We all stand awkwardly, waiting to see who leaves first. I lean in and give very hollow hugs to all three before walking to my car.

Although I wholeheartedly mean to drive back to my house, I somehow find myself in front of my childhood home. A sprawling mansion of gray stone and ivy-covered walls, the entrance is flanked by towering columns and iron gates that stand open as if inviting me in. The front lawn is a meticulously manicured expanse of emerald grass bordered by flower beds bursting with bright colors. The front door, crafted from rich mahogany and intricate carvings, seems like something out of a horror movie, begging me to come in. Above it, a decorative balcony overlooks the entrance.

I pick up my phone from the middle cup holder and press Campbell's number. I listen to it ring on a loop until the sound of his voicemail floods my ears. I hang up, not bothering to leave a message, shut off the ignition, and step outside my car. I'm gripping the key to their house so tight I feel it cutting into my palm, but I can't help it. Everything about this house feels like a loaded gun.

Once I make it inside, I roam around, not knowing what I am looking for. My hands dust over my father's bar cart that's been untouched since he died. I open the cap of his most expensive bottle. He never let me touch his bourbon, but Pappy Van Winkle was especially off-limits. I grab a glass from the cart, pour about two fingers' worth in a cup, and down the whole thing in one gulp. I prefer my bourbon on the rocks, but the defiance makes it smoother. I pour another two-fingers' worth and continue my path down the hallway.

I don't know why I hesitate when I get to my parents' room, but I can't help but be anxious about what's behind the walls of the mother I barely knew. I down the rest of my drink and turn the knob. As the door swings open, it reveals a room that looks like it could be straight out of a high-end interior design magazine. The space is sleek and modern with walls painted in a soft, neutral taupe, contrasting sharply with the crisp white crown molding. The king-size bed, with a tufted headboard in rich gray velvet, dominates the room.

The room smells unmistakably of my mother's signature Chanel No. 5, a comforting and haunting scent. When I finally reach her closet, I walk along the back wall, my hands running across the impeccably curated clothing collection. I make it to her shoes and curse her silently for having feet a size smaller than mine—she has some stunning heels that I would have loved to inherit.

I notice two shoeboxes on the top shelf that stand out amongst the neatly organized rows of clear acrylic displays. I reach up, stretching as tall as I can on my tiptoes, my fingers grazing the boxes. With a final push, they topple over, the contents spilling out.

"Eep," I yelp as the scattered items tumble over my head. I glance down at the mess on the floor and spot several identical small black notebooks among the wreckage.

"I swear to God, if this is some sort of kill list, I'm going to be so pissed," I mutter, grabbing the first notebook within reach, and flipping it open to a random page.

February 19th, 1995

I'm pregnant. Again. I don't know how this happened. I don't know how I am here again. This is why he had the vasectomy. Now I have to do it all again, and I think it may kill me.

My eyes flutter to the date. February 1995. This must've been when she found out she was pregnant with me.

I feel my phone buzz in my pocket and slam the book shut. Campbell's name flashes on my screen, and I instinctively hit ignore.

Quickly, I gather the journals spilled on the floor, shove them back in the boxes, and take them with me as I head back out the front door. That's enough of the haunted house for one day.

***

I drive home silently—my thoughts louder than music could drown out. I can't describe what I am feeling. Part of me is numb, and the part of me that can feel only feels anger. I'm angry at my siblings for not caring enough to be a family. I'm mad at my mother for being a shitty parent and then dying and making us just figure it out. I'm mad at my husband for not being a decent enough person to show up today. My body buzzes as I make my way into our apartment. Well, Campbell's apartment. After we got married, he insisted we move into his top-floor penthouse as I was told my penthouse was too 'dressed down.' I didn't mind when I moved in, but walking through the front door now is the same feeling I got when I walked through my mother's front door only a few hours ago. *Haunted.*

When I reach the living room, Campbell is lounging on the custom Italian leather couch, a low hum of sports commentary buzzing from the wall-mounted TV. He's everything you'd expect from a man who's been groomed for wealth his entire life—flawlessly polished, almost unnervingly so. His blond hair, a perfectly styled mix of disheveled and deliberate, gleams under the recessed lighting. The tailored cut of his navy sweater drapes just right, hinting at the personal shopper who probably chose it for him. Even his jeans look expensive—crisp and impossibly well-fitted, like they've never seen the inside of a washing machine.

Campbell reeks of money, not in the gaudy, flashy way but in a quieter, more insidious way—like his cologne alone probably costs more than my entire wardrobe. And yet, the sight of him makes my skin crawl.

I stop beside the breakfast bar, leaning on the counter, waiting for him to say something. Certainly, he's going to say *something*. I didn't expect him to come running, groveling for forgiveness, but I at least expected an apology. A simple *I'm sorry.*

But there's nothing. He sits there, his eyes fixed on the screen, his presence somehow making the entire room feel heavier.

"Campbell," I say, dumbfounded.

He glances over his shoulder like he just noticed I walked in. "Avery, hi. Sorry, the second period just finished." He rises from the couch with the smoothness of someone who never seems rushed, taking a few steps closer.

I hold up my hand, stopping him in his tracks. "Don't come near me. Where the fuck were you today, Campbell?"

He hesitates, his expression blank, the way it always is when he's preparing an excuse. "Work got crazy. Miller from UAL stopped by for an impromptu meeting, and I couldn't leave. He's our biggest client."

"You couldn't say, 'Oh hey, my mother-in-law died, and my wife kind of needs me to be at the funeral'? You think they just wouldn't understand?"

He extends an arm to touch me, but I swat it away. He gives me a look of annoyance. "You're being irrational."

I laugh in disbelief. "Are you kidding me? I'm being irrational for wanting my husband to be there for me?" I throw my hands up. "Oh, how delusional of me."

I can't believe this. I can't believe that after going to my mother's funeral alone he is trying to fight with me.

"You're a dick." My words wreak of anger, and when my eyes meet his, I watch them grow dark.

"You need to get over it, Avery. That job is why we have this"—he waves his hand around the air—"it means we have to sacrifice sometimes."

The anger I've been trying to keep from boiling over all day reaches its limit. My hand swats at the empty bourbon glass next to my hand on the counter, and I watch it fly through the air before falling and shattering across the floor.

"I'm done," I say, breath catching in my throat. The words hit the air before I even realize I mean them—but once they're out, it's like my lungs finally remember how to work.

Campbell looks at me before he shakes his head. "You're not leaving, Avery. You're emotional. Go to sleep. We can talk tomorrow morning."

I scoff. "I'm not staying here. I mean it, Campbell, I'm done. I want a divorce. I'm twenty-eight—I don't need to be this fucking miserable and alone. I won't be my mother."

I start walking to our room and feel him on my heels. "Oh yeah, where are you going to go? What are you going to do? You think I'm just going to let my wife walk out the door and divorce me?"

I snap around. "And what exactly are you going to do to stop me, Camp?"

He stumbles back, raising his hands slightly in surrender. "Avery. Stop. I would never hurt you." He sounds earnest, and I do believe he'd never hurt me physically, but then he takes two quick steps to me and leans in. "But you know what it'll look like if we divorce now? My firm is merging with Leyland & Roth. You think they want a partner who can't hold his own marriage together? And if you think I'm going to let you go without a fight, you don't know me. You don't think I can drag a divorce out? With the lawyers I know?"

I turn back quickly, grabbing a small duffle and a couple of pieces of clothing. I wouldn't spend time packing. I don't want any of it anyway. It all feels wrong now.

I zip the bag and push his shoulder with mine as I reach the door. "Go ahead. I know plenty of lawyers too. I'm done. We are done."

CHAPTER THREE

Avery

By the time I made it to the lobby of our building, Campbell had already removed my access to the car service. I know what he's doing—he's hoping to get a rise out of me and have me storm back up there to yell at him, but I won't give him the satisfaction.

So, after an hour-long Uber ride with a man who smells like refried beans and B.O., I make it to the Four Seasons downtown.

I breathe in the scent of bamboo and cotton as soon as I step into the lobby with my duffle bag and the two shoeboxes filled with my mother's journals. I'm still in my dress from the funeral, and I'm sure I look like a wreck, but I ignore the lobby full of beautiful people who seemingly look like they have their lives together and head to the front desk.

With a huff, I drop the boxes and my bag on the floor and lift my head with a wide, desperate smile, ready to greet the concierge.

"Hi!" I say cheerily, looking down at the gentleman's name tag. "Cedric. Hi, Cedric."

"Hi. Name on the reservation?"

I put my hands on the counters, clasping them together. "I'm actually looking to book a room."

He looks up, his face in annoyance and disgust as he eyes me up and down. "You don't have a reservation?"

"Nope," I say, popping the *p*. "That's why I am looking to book a room now." I try my hardest to keep my sweet demeanor. I know it's hard to get a room at the Four Seasons at the last minute, but I also know they do hold rooms for these purposes—it's a preference, worst-case scenario hold, but at the end of the day the concierges make the call, so I need Cedric to do me a solid.

"It's a Thursday," he says, as though it should mean something to me.

"I know, and I know it's annoying having someone coming in and needing a room at the last minute. But I need a room. Please. Charge me double. Triple. I don't care. I just really need a room."

I hope my eyes and pouty face look as desperate as they feel, but I can't read his face. So I turn it up a notch, pushing my body up onto my tiptoes, letting my cleavage squish together between my crossed arms. *Desperate times call for desperate measures.*

His lips tighten, forming a flat line. "I'm gay," he says flatly.

I fall back onto my heels and groan, throwing my head into my hands, still planted on the front desk.

I groan before looking back up. "Cedric, old buddy, old pal. Please. I will tip you so much money." I resort to bribery. "Haven't I embarrassed myself enough?"

"Name?" He stares, looking at me with the same look of annoyance as before.

"Really?" I say, jumping happily from toe to toe.

"Yes. Because you look sad and pathetic." As he says it, a smirk appears on his face causing the first genuine laugh to come out of my mouth all day.

"You have no idea how sad and pathetic I am. Thank you. My name is Avery Keenan."

"Credit card?"

"Ah, yes." I bend down, grabbing my wallet and handing him my rose gold Amex.

He looks at the card and at his computer and then the card again. "This card says Avery Ryan, not Keenan."

"That's right, Sorry. My credit card has my married name."

"So, do you want Ryan on the reservation?"

"No. Keenan is good." I assume Campbell will wonder where I went and it might be harder for him to track me down if it's under my maiden name.

Cedric looks at me deadpan. "You want the reservation under your maiden name, even though you're married?" he says slowly and judgingly.

"Oh my god, can you just book me a room?" I snap and immediately hear a low laugh coming from next to me. I look to my left and my eyes pan a large body wearing black Nikes, navy blue shorts, and a tight gray v-neck that hugs his arms tightly. My eye catches a glimpse of a vein protruding from his elbow up his bicep while holding his bag. My mouth feels dry, but I have to swallow the extra saliva that forms in my mouth.

"Something funny?" I ask with a little bit of a bite in my voice.

Cedric's eyes bounce between me and the man standing next to me, before continuing to get me booked in.

He laughs again before leaning closer. "I just love admiring a beautiful woman who can put someone in their place, especially Cedric." He slowly places his hand on the counter. "Hope to see you around," he mutters as he walks behind me to move toward the elevators.

I smirk before shouting behind him. "Don't count on it."

***

The quick encounter with the hot mystery stranger at the front desk has my body buzzing in a way that feels foreign after months—no, years—of numbness. *Cedric is right. I am pathetic.* That's the only reason why a random stranger calling me beautiful has me confidently strutting up to my hotel room the night of my mother's funeral, the same night I've left my husband.

The door clicks shut behind me, and I lean against it momentarily, letting the weight of the day press down on me before I push off and head straight for the minibar. Without hesitation, I grab the tiny Jack Daniels' and down it in one swig, pretending the burn relieves the ache in my chest, but it doesn't, it's just a distraction.

I strip down to my bra and underwear, leaving my clothes in a crumpled heap on the floor, and crawl into the oversized bed. I didn't think to pack pajamas in my rush to leave. I figured three outfits would be enough to get me by until I can shop. *Rookie mistake, Avery.*

I toss and turn, the space in the king-size bed feeling impossibly vast. Sleep feels impossible, no matter how hard I try to trick my mind into shutting down. After three more mini bottles of whiskey—each one tasting worse than the last—I'm still painfully awake, the silence of the suite deafening.

Groaning, I sit up and flick on the lamp beside the bed. Its warm glow spills over the room, and I catch sight of the stack of shoeboxes on the other nightstand, the journals inside practically taunting me. I pull the closest box toward me, the cardboard feeling strangely heavy in my hands. My mother's handwriting peeks out from the edges of the books, neat and meticulous. I grab the first journal I see, flipping it open cautiously, almost afraid of what I might find. I don't think I am ready to hear how my mother resented me from the start, but I flip open the book anyway and spot the date: March 1, 1992, and I feel a slight smile on my lips. In 1992, my mother was my age.

March 1, 1992

I am so excited about Daniel and my first anniversary. He is taking me to a seafood bar downtown, and I've been dreaming about their Oyster Rockefeller and dirty martinis for the past month. I've also been dreaming about Daniel's face when he sees me in the lingerie I bought for tonight. It's everything he loves in one little package.

But somewhere between the oysters and the mind-blowing sex, I do need to talk to him about the restaurant plans. My idea is good: a library and wine bar during the day and a speakeasy, high-end restaurant at night. We know the customers. We know the market. I want this, and we can do it together. This feels like the start of our lives.

March 15, 1992

Well, the dinner was terrific, and I've been drinking dirty martinis every day since to keep the spark alive. There is something powerful about a dirty martini. The boys can keep their warm, overpriced scotch. I'll stick with an ice-cold vodka martini and three perfectly skewered olives.

We also discussed business and agreed to focus on the hotel plans this year. Next year, we will start planning and taking the next steps for the restaurant, which is perfect because it gives me a year to strategize and be prepared. Things are starting to fall into place.

Oh yeah, and the anniversary sex was incredible.

I close the book and look ahead, zoning out in my thoughts. She sounds so hopeful and happy. Where did it all go wrong?

March 1992 must've been right before she got pregnant with Abigail. I sigh, not knowing what to think. If she didn't want us, why did she keep having kids? Why four kids in four years when you had all these goals and ambitions for something else? Especially when it made her miserable.

I set the book back in the box, turn off the light, and force myself to sleep, dreaming of dirty martinis.

Chapter Four

Chase

When my apartment flooded six weeks ago, I figured living in a hotel would suck. Cold hallways, stiff sheets, overpriced room service. But honestly? It's not that bad. The bed's decent, housekeeping leaves chocolates on my pillow, and the guy at the front desk—Cedric—treats me like I'm royalty. I've been on the road so much I barely notice the difference.

And then last night happened.

This woman checked in. Total chaos wrapped in a perfect storm—loud, flustered, fighting tooth-and-nail with Cedric over a room. Most people would crumble under that kind of pressure, but not her. She handled it like a champ. Funny, sarcastic, confident. She had this energy that made it impossible to look away.

And those eyes—holy hell. Deep green, like some enchanted forest you want to get lost in. I swear I forgot how to breathe when she looked at me. I tossed out a casual line, fully expecting to be brushed off. Instead, she smirked and tossed it right back, smooth as hell. I've been thinking about that exchange ever since. As a forward for the New York Devils, I've had my fair share of encounters with the opposite sex, and not to be cocky but there aren't many that walk away from my flirting easily. Though, from what I could hear between her and Cedric, it sounds like her current relationship could be complicated.

But that's why I always say, anything serious before your thirties is a waste of time. No one is on the same page, no one wants to settle down. Everyone wants the glamor and shine, and none of the commitment or actual love involved. So I follow suit, throwing my love into hockey and my friends, and I appreciate the hookups with the beautiful women along the way. And hey, maybe everyone is right, because with all the women I've been with—hook-up or relationship-wise—in the past, it never felt...right.

Growing up, I watched my parents be insanely in love with each other. Like grossly in love, making out in the kitchen when they thought my brothers and sisters and I were upstairs, laughing in their bedroom late into the night, and doing at-home date nights when we were too young and they couldn't afford babysitters. It wasn't until I was in my early twenties that I realized what they had. My parents were best friends first, married second, and parents third. They were a team. A unit. And they made sure that we knew all of us were one team together. But I've never truly felt like part of a team with anyone besides the Devils, and I refuse to settle for anything less than being in love with my best friend.

When my dad died last year, it sent a shockwave through my whole family, but my siblings stepped up for my mom while I was still in season. Now, during the off-season, I go back to Boston as much as possible and FaceTime with them often. My twin sisters, Sara and Meghan, are still in high school, so my mom is distracted in taming their wild ways. Derek lives in Boston with his wife, and they all still have dinner every Sunday. Slowly, we are figuring out how to keep living. When my dad first got sick, he made sure to tell us what he wanted when he passed. He didn't want us to be sad, mourning his loss. He wanted us to live, be happy, and make him proud. So, every day I get up and find happiness and live in a way that I think would make him proud.

Today, that includes sitting in a hotel bar watching a live MMA fight like we used to. Now, it's just me and the TV, but I still hear his commentary in my head. Whenever someone throws a weak punch, I hear him grunt, "That all you got, champ?"

The bar's quiet tonight. Low lights, a few patrons murmuring over overpriced cocktails, and the fight already playing on the screen above me. I order a beer and settle in, eyes glued to the screen. I've got a thousand bucks on Tony Kee knocking out Buckers in the first round, and right now, it's not looking promising.

Then, boom.

Kee lands a vicious right hook, and Buckers drops like a sack of bricks. First-round knockout. Just like I predicted.

"Let's go!" I say under my breath, raising my beer in a silent toast to myself.

"He's pretty good, huh?"

That voice.

I glance over and nearly choke on my drink. It's her. The hotel mystery girl. She slides onto the stool next to mine like she owns the place. Loose hair, subtle makeup, but somehow still looking like she stepped out of a dream.

"Well, if it isn't the mystery girl with the last-minute reservation. I was hoping to see you again." My smirk growing by the second.

"I prefer Avery, but mystery girl works too," she says, revealing her name.

Avery. Suits her.

I break out of my trance and realize she's staring at me, waiting for me to introduce myself. "Chase. I'm Chase," I stutter. *What is happening right now? Am I fourteen years old?*

A slight smirk breaks out on her face. "Damn, I love that name."

This gives me a boost of confidence. "You should get to know the rest of me," I say smugly, glancing down at my crotch.

She laughs off my misogynistic joke, and I chuckle along with her. The bartender walks up with my steak and sets it in front of me.

"Are those mashed potatoes?" Avery asks, desire laced in her voice.

"Even better, they're truffle mashed potatoes."

"Oh my god. Can I have the exact same thing he's having?" She directs her question to the bartender standing in front of us.

"Of course, ma'am. How would you like your steak prepared?" he asks.

"Medium rare, please," she replies, her voice full of genuine gratitude.

"Of course. Anything to drink?"

She pauses, thinking about what she wants to drink before answering. "Can I do a dirty martini with three olives, please?"

"Coming up." He turns his attention to me. "Another beer, sir?"

"Yes, please. Thanks," I respond, my eyes not leaving Avery. Once he walks away, I return my full attention to her. "Medium rare. Again, a girl after my own heart."

While she waits for her food, I slide my plate over to her. She blinks, surprised.

"Seriously?"

"You're hungry. I've got time." I flash a grin. "Besides, I'm a giver."

She laughs, shaking her head as she digs in. That laugh? It does something to me. It's not forced or polite. It's real—from the belly, with a little snort at the end. The kind of laugh that makes you want to keep cracking jokes just to hear it again.

She smiles as she takes a bite, and a few minutes later the bartender comes and sets her martini and steak in front of me.

"So, tell me about yourself, mystery girl," I say as I let the first bite of my steak melt into my mouth. I have to suppress a moan. Another benefit of living in a hotel, specifically the Four Seasons, is the best steak and beer in the city.

"No thanks," she replies, and I chuckle.

"Don't like sharing about yourself?" I tease.

"I just don't see the point of sharing my favorite color or food with a hot stranger," she says, and once again a smile takes over my face.

"So, you think I'm hot."

Her cheeks pinken and she looks down at her food, pushing a bite of potatoes back and forth, and then she shocks me by turning and locking eyes. "You know you're hot."

"Fine. How about this: two truths and a lie? I'll go first."

She nods reluctantly and I continue. "One: I currently live at the Four Seasons. Two: I play for the NHL. Three: I hate wasabi."

She laughs as I overemphasize the word "hate" and then looks at my face studying it, hoping my face will give away which lie it is. Her eyes twinkle. She leans a little closer and says, "You love wasabi."

She leans back, and I mimic her body movements. "You're good." I nod. "Now it's your turn."

She rolls her lips in as she thinks and then begins her list. "One: I'm an event planner. Two: I'm getting a divorce. Three: I love wasabi."

Now I take a moment to study her, although I already know the lie. As soon as she finishes, I use the opportunity to lean forward, brushing my hand across her arm, moving her long brown hair out of the way so I can whisper in her ear. "You hate wasabi."

She sucks in a quick breath, almost unnoticeable, and leans back. And again, I do the same, never taking my eyes off of her.

"Okay. One point for each of us. My turn again. One: I'm a goalie for the NHL. Two: I have three siblings. Three: I'm obsessed with golden retrievers, completely fanboy obsessed."

A soft laugh falls from her lips, and I feel like I've already become addicted to the sound. "Hmm," she hums. "I don't know much about hockey, but you don't look like a goalie."

"You'd be correct." I nod. "But really? You don't like hockey? That's a travesty."

"I'm into more solo sports—gymnastics, golf, those kinds of things."

"Okay, okay. I can understand that. But you should give it a chance when the season starts back up. Oh. Now I have another one for my next round," I say, thinking about the bet I won earlier. "Go, go." I wave my hand, moving her along eagerly.

She sighs, but her smile grows. The bartender reappears before she can start her turn, asking if we're interested in another round. I'm about to say yes, but she turns, grabbing her phone off the counter for the first time since she's sat down, and frowns. She tosses her phone into her purse and turns her attention back to us, and says, "I should call it a night."

A wave of disappointment rushes through me, and I'm not quite sure why, but I've never been one to question my instincts.

"Can you put this on my room?" She waves over her empty plate and martini glass.

"Of course, ma'am."

I look at the bartender and ask, "Can I borrow a pen and a piece of paper?"

He nods, handing me a pen and a light green sticky note. I scribble my number on it quickly and stand up at the same time she does. She barely reaches my chin when we're standing, which is adorable.

Her eyes flutter up to meet mine. "Thanks for the company. It was fun."

I grab her hand, bring it to the middle of us, and place the sticky note into her palm. "If you want to finish the game."

She smiles, looks down at the number and then back up at me. "Chase," she says, and I can't help but love the sound of my name coming out of her mouth. "My truth earlier...I am getting a divorce, but it's new. Like, a couple of days new. So it would probably be better if we didn't."

That does sound messy, and usually I'd walk away to avoid any of that drama, but all of my instincts say not to, so instead I close her hand so she's clasping the sticky note. "It's just a game, mystery girl."

And I walk away from her for the second time in twenty-four hours.

CHAPTER FIVE

Avery

The day's weight crashes down on me the moment I step into my hotel room. I don't even bother with the lights, I just throw myself onto the bed face first into the pillows and let out a muffled groan. The faint scent of fresh linen is oddly comforting.

My phone buzzes on the nightstand, an insistent vibration that's impossible to ignore. I turn my head, squinting at the screen. Eight missed calls from Campbell and a dozen unread texts piling up like little time bombs. I know I should call him back, face the mess head-on, but the thought alone sends a wave of exhaustion through me. Between my mother's funeral, walking away from my marriage, and trying to figure out what the hell comes next, I'm barely holding it together.

The only relief is this amazing bed, endless room service, and the unexpected distraction of a particular gorgeous hockey player I keep running into at the hotel. I feel like I'm in a game of cat and mouse. I look for him when I go to the gym or pool, in the lobby, or at the bar restaurant, but whenever I catch a glimpse of him, I hide like I'm a teenager again.

I never texted him because I was right when I told him my divorce was brand new. I mean, hell, I haven't even reached out to a lawyer yet; I've just been hiding out for a week, buying an entirely new wardrobe, cutting over eight inches off my hair, and binge-drinking dirty martinis every night. It's not the right time for anything new—even harmless flirting with a hot pro athlete.

Except now I haven't seen him in three days, and it's driving me crazy. Did he check out of the hotel? He told me he lives here, but it has to be temporary. I have been stalking the bar each night, hoping to catch a glimpse of him, and nothing. I even got so desperate that I tried to get the information out of Cedric, but he might as well be a CIA agent. He would just repeat that he doesn't share other guests' information. Damn rule-follower.

I head to the hotel bar for the fourth night in a row, silently hoping to find Chase there. As usual, I'm met with disappointment. A middle-aged couple occupies the far end, an older gentleman sits in the middle, and scattered tables are filled with couples and families.

I huff and sink into my usual seat as Steven, the bar-tender, approaches. I learned his name on my first night searching for Chase. That night, he served me three dirty martinis, a Diet Coke, and a loaf of bread before making sure I made it back to my floor. Since then, he's become a companion, and I've given him advice about his long-distance girlfriend.

"I haven't seen him tonight," Steven says, shaking his head in sympathy.

Without needing to ask, he starts making my martini and looks up. "Food tonight?" he asks, though his tone suggests he's more concerned about me drinking on an empty stomach than anything else.

"How about the steak and truffle potatoes?"

He smiles, places my drink in front of me, and heads to his computer to put in my order.

My phone buzzes with a call from Campbell. I sigh, swipe to answer, and put the phone to my ear. "Campbell," I say, my voice flat.

"Avery. Thank god. Where the hell have you been?" His voice is urgent, a mix of relief and desperation, as if he can't believe I answered and is afraid I'll hang up any moment.

"I'm at a hotel. I'm fine. I just need some time," I reply, not wanting to delve into details right now.

"We need to talk—face-to-face. You're my wife. You owe me a conversation before you just run away and disappear."

"I didn't run away, Campbell. I told you I was leaving and walked out the door. You could have followed me and made some effort. Instead, you didn't show up at my mother's funeral, tried to downplay it, and let me walk away."

He doesn't respond, only repeats himself. "You're my wife."

"Not for long," I say, pulling the phone away from my ear and ending the call. I pick up my martini, slide the toothpick with the olives out, and bite into the first one.

I take my phone and the light green sticky note from my purse, typing a quick text.

> **Me:** 1. I cut my hair for the first time in over five years this week. 2. I haven't had a sip of alcohol all week. 3. I'm bummed I haven't seen you in days and wondering if you've checked out of the hotel.

His reply comes through almost immediately, and for some reason it makes me smile.

> **Chase:** I knew you'd miss me. I'm at my mom's this week, my last big visit before preseason starts. I'm driving back tomorrow.

My fingers hover over my phone, trying to decide how to respond when another text arrives.

> **Chase:** I should be in by 7. Any chance you'll be at the bar then?

I grin and open my camera, taking a picture of myself with the bar and Steven bustling around in the background, then send it to him.

> **Me:** I would count on it.

> **Chase:** Your hair looks amazing.

> **Me:** It's better in person.

> **Chase:** I have no doubt.

I set my phone down and focus on the plate Steven just placed in front of me. I take a bite of my steak when my phone buzzes again.

> **Chase:** So it's my turn. 1. Growing up I always thought I'd play football, but in eighth grade, I put skates on for the first time, and I swear I never wanted to take them off. 2. I constantly feel like I could be doing more. I could be working harder, trying new things, IDK. I just have a hard time staying still. 3. I hate the show Friends. Terrible. Not funny at all.

> **Me:** I sincerely hope #3 is a lie, or we have no shot at being friends.

A moment later, Chase sends a picture of himself on the couch with the TV in the background, clearly showing Joey and Rachel.

> **Me:** Good boy.

Three dots appear, then disappear, and another picture arrives—Chase with his arm around a middle-aged woman with short blonde hair and a warm smile. She looks just like him.

Chase: Jesus, Avery. You can't call me a good boy while I'm with my mom and a hundred miles away from you.

I laugh as I type my reply.

Me: What can I say? I'm passionate about Friends.

Chase: What else are you passionate about?

Me: Sometimes I feel like I have no idea.

Me: Can that be one of my truths?

Chase: Absolutely. What else?

I hesitate, my fingers hovering over the screen. I almost tell him about the journals. About how I've been reading through my mother's handwritten confessions like they're a roadmap to understanding how our family ended up so broken. I almost tell him that I found out she was pregnant with me and wanted to scream, not celebrate. That her voice, even written in ink, still manages to make me feel like I was always one mistake too many.

But I don't. Because that's too much. So instead, I send him a truth that's a little raw, but not bleeding.

Me: I desperately need to leave the hotel bar as I'm on my third martini…again.

> **Me:** And 3. I did not look up your stats from last season.

As I wait for his response, I ask Steven to put my food and drinks on my room tab and prepare to leave. Just as I'm about to stand up, my phone rings.

Chase.

"Hello?" I answer, confused.

"Need a friendly voice while you get to your room?"

I give Steven a quick nod and goodbye and start walking toward the elevator. "You know I'm not some damsel in distress, right? And I'm six floors away from my room."

"Oh, so you're on the sixth floor. What number?"

I open my mouth to say my room number—6005—but stop, staying silent.

Chase chuckles on the other end, sending a warm buzz through me.

"So you've been looking me up, huh?"

"I stumbled upon your stats if that's what you mean. They're..." I pause, searching for the right word. "Adequate."

"Bullshit. My stats are stellar," he replies confidently.

"They're all right," I joke back, and he laughs again.

The elevator dings and opens on the sixth floor. "I just got to my floor. I should go," I say, not wanting to hang up but feeling like every conversation inches us closer to dangerous territory.

"Wait, wait," he says eagerly. "I have to take my turn."

I smile, balancing my phone between my ear and shoulder while retrieving my key and unlocking my door.

I flick the lights on, put my phone on speaker, and toss it on the bed. "Okay, go," I say, pulling off my shorts and removing my leotard top, leaving me in my black bra and panties. I sit on the bed, feeling the effects of the martinis and Chase's voice.

"One: I hate roller coasters. Two: I found out a couple of days ago that my apartment won't be done for another eight weeks. Three: The last time I had a serious girlfriend was in high school."

I hold my breath. "Which is the lie?" my voice barely whispers.

"One."

"Why?"

"Well, I went to Cedar Point every year as a kid and..."

I cut him off. "You know that's not what I was talking about," I groan.

"Is saying I haven't met the right person too cliché?" His voice is earnest.

"Yes. Come on, you gotta give me more than that."

There's a pause, shifting sheets fill the silence, followed by a soft sigh. I can almost picture him lying back on his bed, stretching out. I can hear the rustle of his comforter, the way he adjusts himself, settling into a rhythm. He's getting comfortable. I wait for his answer, listening as he shifts again, his voice now more casual, like he's physically relaxing but mentally still with me, trying to figure out how to open up without feeling exposed.

"Growing up, I watched my parents be insanely in love—just absolute best friends who would do anything for each other. It set this impossible standard, you know?

I've never felt that way with anyone. I have this saying, *any relationship before thirty isn't worth it*. It feels like everyone's on different pages."

I absorb his words carefully. "Parents in love, huh? Are they still together?"

He's silent for a moment, then says, "My dad died a little over a year ago."

His sadness is raw and emotional, and I wonder if my voice sounds similar when I talk about my parents or if it's more monotone and numb.

"I'm sorry," I reply, my voice soft.

"Thanks," he says quietly.

I roll onto my side, the phone wedged between my ear and pillow. "How about your parents?" he asks.

"Dead," I say bluntly, then hesitate. "I don't really know how they felt about each other. It wasn't what I imagined love to be like."

The line goes quiet again and I press on to fill the space. "Sorry. I haven't figured out how to answer questions about my parents politely yet."

"When did they die?" His tone is careful, almost hesitant, like he's afraid to push too hard.

"My dad, a couple of years ago. My mom...last week."

"Last week?" he repeats, disbelief weaving through his words.

"Yeah. Her funeral was the day I checked into the hotel."

"Avery," he says softly, his voice thick with sympathy. "I am so sorry."

"It's fine," I say quickly, not wanting to delve deeper. Instead, I switch topics with a teasing lilt in my voice. "So...eight more weeks stuck at the Four Seasons. What's the plan?"

He chuckles lightly, the shift in tone a welcome reprieve. "That really depends. How long will *you* be there?"

I laugh, the sound soft and fleeting. "Forever. Or at least until I find an apartment, whichever comes first. But honestly, after the first week, I'm starting to like living in a hotel. I feel like Eloise."

"I love that movie!" he exclaims, and the enthusiasm in his voice makes me smile.

"Me too." I sigh, my voice softening with the weight of exhaustion creeping in. I yawn, covering the phone instinctively even though he can't see me. "I should get some sleep. I have a very important bar date tomorrow."

"Huh, funny. So do I," he says, his voice playful but quieter now, as though we're both unwilling to let the conversation end.

For a brief moment, I think about saying *never mind* to sleep, staying up just to talk to him longer. But instead, I smile into the pillow and say, "Good night."

"Good night, mystery girl. I'll see you tomorrow."

He hangs up first. I stare at the screen for a moment before setting my phone on the bed.

I stand, pull on my pajamas, the soft fabric brushing against my skin as I head to the bathroom. The mirror reflects tired eyes and a weary smile as I wash my face and brush my teeth. When I return to bed, my gaze falls on the small box perched on the nightstand. My hand hovers over it, hesitating before I reach for the journal at the top of the stack. The cover is smooth under my fingers as I flip it open.

April 3, 1992

I'm pregnant.

I can't believe I am writing that down, and it's real—I am pregnant.

I just took the test and the two thin lines showed up imme-diately. I cried and laughed and then cried some more, and then I ran to the store, bought a plain onesie, and decorated it with glitter pens.

I plan to give it to Daniel when he gets home from work—he's going to think it's hideous, but I hope he's as happy as I am.

***

Were my parents in love like Chase's parents? And if so, what happened? Why did we grow up the way we did if this is how it started?

I shut the book, hating the idea that all love is bound to end disastrously, but then my phone rings and Camp-bell's name appears, and I realize maybe it's just reality.

CHAPTER SIX

Chase

I zip up my bag, pausing to look around my childhood room. The soft morning light filters through the curtains, casting a warm glow over the room. As I head down the stairs, the rich aroma of bacon fills the air, mingling with the faint scent of freshly brewed coffee. I can't help but groan inwardly, the smell is almost too inviting, making it even harder to leave.

Entering the kitchen, I find my sisters huddled at the counter, their heads bent over their phones. They're deep in conversation, their eyes glued to the screens, barely acknowledging my presence. With a playful smirk, I gently tap each of their heads as I walk by.

"Hey, I'm your brother, the one who's leaving. Just thought I'd remind you to pay attention to me," I tease.

I walk over to the island where my mom stands, her face illuminated by the morning sun. She's already dishing out a plate piled high with golden bacon, fluffy pancakes, and scrambled eggs. She hands me the plate with a warm smile, and I wrap my arm around her, kissing her cheek.

"Thanks, Mom."

Her smile widens, a mixture of pride and affection in her eyes. "Of course, honeybun."

I smile at the endearing nickname and sit at the table across from my sisters, who have finally looked up from their phones. Their eyes briefly meet mine before they drop to the plate of food in front of me.

Sarah raises an eyebrow and asks, "How are you possibly going to eat all that?"

I lean back in my chair, rubbing my stomach with mock seriousness. "I'm a growing boy."

My mom rolls her eyes and sits beside me. "How's the hotel? I worry about you being there."

"Mom, you don't need to worry," I reassure her. "The Four Seasons is about as nice as it can get. It's comfortable, and the staff is great."

She sighs a touch of anxiety in her voice. "I just worry you're lonely."

I chuckle lightly. "It's not like I had roommates before my place flooded, so there are more people around me now than before. Plus, tonight I'm meeting up with someone else who's staying at the hotel."

My mom and sisters straightened up immediately, their interest piqued. Their eyes widen as my mom asks, "You have a date?"

"No, no. It's not a date," I clarify quickly. "We both happen to live at the hotel, and we're..." I pause, searching for the right word but opting for the safest choice. "Friends."

Just then, my brother walks into the kitchen. Both of my sisters, caught up in the moment, shout in unison. "Chase has a date!"

Their synchronized exclamation fills the room with a mix of surprise and amusement. Derek looks at me with a raised eyebrow as if to ask if it's true.

I roll my eyes, getting up from my seat.

"Derek, you're just in time. I have to go."

We hug and I keep holding on. "I'll miss you, brother. Where's the wife?"

He smiles and squeezes me tighter. "I'll miss you too, kid. She's good. She had work or would have been here to see you off."

"No worries, man, but I better see you both at the preseason opener next month."

"Of course. We are making a whole weekend out of it."

"Good," I say, smiling back.

After saying goodbye, I get into my beat-up 2006 Ford Bronco and start my three-hour drive. I never drive in the city, but this car has been with me since I started driving at sixteen, and I fully intend to ride it until the wheels fall off. Before I get too far out of town, I stop at a gas station to fill up and grab a Diet Coke. I buckle my seatbelt back up and put my car into drive, but quickly shift back to park. I pick my phone up, text Avery quickly, letting her know I'm leaving and will be on time, and then start my drive with only one thing on my mind: Drinks at seven.

$$***$$

I make it back to the city by three in the afternoon and head straight to the rink for our preseason meeting. With practice starting next week, this is when we get our preseason schedules and discuss any events we need to plan for.

As I stroll past the rink toward the elevators, my steps slow as the rink comes into view. The sight of the freshly Zambonied ice stops me in my tracks. The ice is perfect, untouched, pulling me into a familiar spell. It's my absolute favorite view—the glassy surface gleaming like a frozen mirror under the arena lights, every reflection sharp and pristine. The faint hum of the arena's machinery is the only sound, a steady background melody that can calm all my nerves in seconds.

Reluctantly, I pull myself away, turning toward the elevators and riding them to the top floor where our VIP suites and conference room are situated.

I exchange a few nods with my teammates as I go through the corridor, heading toward where I see my three best friends standing.

When I joined the Devils two years ago, I wasn't worried about making friends. If nothing else, I am a team player, which tends to attract at least some people who want to be friends. What I didn't expect was to meet the three best friends I've ever had.

Riley Towns, the team captain, embodies leadership and dedication. He tells anyone who will listen that he put skates on when he was three years old and never looked back. He is a natural leader. Off the ice, Riley's newly married to a girl I absolutely love, who is the perfect match for him. Both of them are insanely loyal and have the best sense of humor. They are always the first to offer support or a well-timed joke to lift our spirits.

James Towns, Riley's younger brother and the best goalie in the league, was born into a hockey family, and this is shown through his sharp reflexes and his ability to stay calm under pressure in every game. Despite his intense focus on the ice, James has a laid-back, approachable side that makes him easy to talk to and always up for a laugh. He is a notorious playboy, but he also has this superhuman ability to be legitimate friends with all his exes or past hookups. I genuinely do not understand it, but I love watching it happen.

And finally, Billy Baker is a skilled defenseman known for his quick wit and infectious enthusiasm. His energy on the ice is unmatched, and he is the only guy I know who can get a group of men hyped when we are losing with five minutes left in a period. He is serial monogamous but recently got out of a long relationship and has been trying the dating game. It's failing hilariously.

"Gentleman," I greet them with a slap on James' back as I come up behind him.

"Chase, you bastard. Where've you been?" James laughs while turning to hug me.

"Last chance for a weekend back at my mom's before the season."

I watch Riley nod knowingly. I'd like to say he knows that just because we're good friends, but he keeps tabs on all the players. Like I said, he is a great captain.

"How long do you think this will take?" Billy's voice is monotone, and I glance at Riley and James.

"Is this guy still sulking?" I say, throwing a thumb in Billy's direction.

"Dude, don't even get him started," James groans, making me laugh.

"We are going to Shakers after this to help Billy lick his wounds. Again. You in?"

I'm about to say yes when my mind flashes to Avery's smile. "Nah. Not tonight."

"You just got back to town and don't even have a home. How do you have plans?"

I stare at the guys, unsure how to say I'm meeting with a woman I met at the hotel and can't stop thinking about her, but luckily, our coach and GM walking through the door interrupts me.

"*Gentlemen, listen up.*" The coach's voice echoes through the hallway. "File into the conference room, sit down, and we'll make this quick and painless."

We file into the room and settle into our seats like overgrown toddlers. Our GM steps up to the front of the room with a stack of folders. His presence commands attention, and everyone quiets down immediately.

"All right, everyone," our GM starts, his tone brisk but with a hint of enthusiasm. "We have three important charity events coming up before the season starts."

Neil Declan, our general manager, is a massive advocate for two things in this world: hockey and charity work. He's like many people who came from poverty and worked his ass off, and now makes an easy seven figures a year, if not more. Instead of being greedy and spending money on all the things he didn't have, he genuinely helps the community, and he doesn't stand for any players who don't have the same attitude. I've seen him trade guys who try to get out of charity work or talk in any ill light of the work we do.

"The first is the annual Youth Hockey Clinic, where we'll work with kids from local schools to teach them the game basics and offer some guidance. It's always a great time and a fantastic way to give back to the community."

He pauses for a moment, flipping through the folders. "Next, we have the charity gala, our yearly formal charity event to raise funds for local underprivileged youth programs. It's an opportunity to put on our best suits and make a real impact with our presence. And finally, there's the third event, which..." He pauses, continuing to scan the papers. "We don't know what that is yet."

Neil looks up, meeting each of our eyes. "We've got interviews this week for the event planners who will help us organize these events. We'll know more details after that, but I wanted to give you a heads-up so you can mark your calendars and start planning your availability.

No excuses and no misses unless you or someone you know—that I like—is dying."

Riley gives a nod of approval, clearly already planning how he'll support leading these events. James mutters something about buying a new suit for the gala while Billy rolls his eyes but doesn't dare look uninterested.

Neil claps his hands together and wraps up the meeting. "All right, that's it from me. Coach has preseason practice updates, and then you can get out of here and enjoy what's left of your day. Remember, these events are important so let's make sure we show up ready to give our best."

As Neil mentioned, Coach comes up, runs through the schedules emailed to us earlier that morning, and discusses picking up our personalized meal plans next week and new equipment updates. The meeting finally wraps up a little before six, and the only thing on my mind is getting back to the hotel room, showering, and heading to the bar to meet Avery.

By the time I make it to the hotel, my body is buzzing with excitement to see her, and I have to shake my head and bring myself back to reality. I just met this girl, and she is technically still married, but every part of me is getting pulled to her. And right now, I'm not willing to walk away without figuring out why.

My eyes scan the front desk and I spot Cedric standing behind it. Instead of his usual overly friendly customer service demeanor, he's wearing a tight, concerned expression. With no guests around, I walk up to him. "You okay, man?"

Cedric meets my gaze briefly before his eyes dart toward the bar and then back to me. *Weird.*

"What's going on?" I ask again, and he shakes his head quickly.

"Nothing, nothing. Welcome back. Do you need another room key?"

I give him a curious look but shrug it off. Cedric is an interesting guy—I once saw him after the hotel got a bad Yelp review and he looked like someone had just stolen his cat. It was dark.

"Uh, yeah. I actually do," I reply, realizing I left my room key in my room when I left last week.

Cedric keeps glancing toward the bar and then back at me. "Is there some sort of mob gathering happening at the bar, man? What's up?" I laugh, but Cedric's expression remains unchanged.

"Are you planning to go to the bar?" he asks.

"I was planning to come down in an hour, but you're freaking me out, so now I don't want to," I say, my voice tinged with humor and sarcasm.

"Why don't you just go now?"

I look at the multiple bags I'm holding and then back at him. "Uh, my hands are a little full, and I'd like to shower."

"I can hold your bags. You go," Cedric says, already moving from behind the desk and grabbing my bags. He tugs them away from me and I reluctantly let go. "This is weird, man."

"Yeah, yeah, just go," Cedric insists, shooing me away.

My mind races with questions about Cedric's strange behavior, but everything becomes apparent as soon as I step into the bar. Avery is standing next to her usual seat, seemingly yelling at a man in a suit. My feet freeze as I watch her. She hasn't noticed me, and I can't quite make out every word she's saying as I'm still across the room.

I stay rooted to the spot, every muscle in my body coiled with tension as I watch the scene unfold. Who the hell is this guy? My mind races, trying to piece together what I'm seeing. Is he her ex? A coworker? Just some random guy she's arguing with? Either way, it shouldn't matter. I'm just a hotel guest, a guy who chats with her at the bar. This isn't my business. It has nothing to do with me.

But then he grabs her arm.

The movement is sharp, aggressive. She stiffens, her body jerking slightly as he tugs her closer. Her face doesn't show fear, not yet, but there's a flicker of something—a flash of discomfort, of resistance—that ignites something primal inside me.

Suddenly, my mind blanks and the world narrows. My pulse pounds in my ears, drowning out the low hum of the bar's background noise. The dim lighting, the murmur of conversation, the clinking of glasses—all of it fades as my vision tunnels on her and the guy with his hand on her arm.

Red washes over my vision, anger sears through my veins. Before I even realize it my feet are moving. My strides are long, purposeful, and unstoppable. The air around me seems to crackle with tension as I close the distance between us. I can't think—I can only act.

My hand clamps down on the guy's shoulder, hard enough to make my intention crystal clear, and I shove him backward. He stumbles, arms flailing as he collides with the stools behind him. For a second, I pause, part of me hoping he'll topple completely and give me the satisfaction of watching him hit the floor. But no. He grips the edge of a stool and steadies himself, his face twisting into anger and embarrassment.

"Grab her again, I dare you." The words come out low and venomous, fueled by the steady burn of adrenaline coursing through me. My fists tighten at my sides, ready for whatever comes next.

"What the fuck?" he barks, straightening up and taking a step toward me. Bold move. Ballsy, but bold.

I shift to the right, placing myself fully between him and Avery. My shoulders square, my stance solid, like I'm a wall he'll have to get through to even glance her way. But I still can't bring myself to turn and look at her—not yet.

"Who the fuck is this 'roided-up asshole?" he sneers, craning his neck to look past me at Avery.

The steroid comment stings less than it should. If nothing else, it's a backhanded compliment. This muscle? Hard-earned. Clean. And I will show him that if he takes another step toward Avery.

"The better question," I counter, my voice like ice, "is who the fuck are you? And why do you think you can grab a woman like that?"

I know the answer before I even finish the question. I noticed it the second he grabbed her—the flash of gold on his left hand—a wedding band. And yet, hearing the confirmation in his voice as he spits his reply hits harder than I expected.

"I'm her fucking husband," he snaps, his words slicing through the air like a blade.

CHAPTER SEVEN

Avery

"I'm her fucking husband."

I've never felt more like a piece of property. My body has already broken out into a sweat because the second Chase ripped Campbell off me, my body felt on fire in all the best ways. Now, it feels dirty and cold.

I lift my gaze to meet Campbell's eyes, only to quickly look away toward Chase. We are all silent, the tension building by the second. As I scan the bar, I realize that not only Steven but everyone in the bar is watching us with intrigue. My gaze darts to Cedric standing anxiously in the entryway, and my pulse quickens. My fight or flight senses are kicking in, just like at my mother's funeral not even two weeks ago, but instead of running I take in a deep breath and turn my focus back to Campbell.

"You need to leave," I say, my voice trembling despite my efforts to sound firm.

"I'm not going anywhere," Campbell responds almost instantly.

Chase steps forward but I instinctively grab his arm, pulling him back. His eyes snap to mine, and I give him a desperate look, pleading for him to hold back. I need to get out of here, and that will only be delayed if they get into a full-blown fight.

He hesitates but then steps back, positioning himself slightly in front of me, and my body instinctively floods with heat again.

What the hell is happening to me?

"Campbell. Leave," I repeat, trying to maintain steady eye contact.

Campbell glances around the room, taking in the collective scrutiny. His eyes shift from mine to Chase's, and after a moment of stubborn hesitation, he shakes his head. "We'll talk soon."

I don't respond but watch as he strides toward the entryway. Cedric scurries away, quickly retreating to the front desk, and I finally release the breath I had been holding since Campbell walked in.

After another minute of standing in silence, I look down and realize I'm still holding onto Chase's hand. I quickly drop it, but immediately miss the warmth.

"Sooo," I drag out. "That's my ex-husband."

"Seems like a real asshole," Chase replies, looking down at me.

"Yep. Tell me about it." I still can't bring myself to meet his gaze, and I'm baffled by why he isn't rushing away now that Campbell is gone. If he's staying, then I sure as hell am leaving.

Summoning the courage, I finally look up at him. He looks exhausted, and an overwhelming urge to wrap my arms around him. But I force myself to stay put and speak. "I know we had plans, but"—I gesture around the room—"I think this kind of ruined it. Can we maybe reschedule?"

"Yeah, of course," he replies, his voice soothing and calm. But I'm under no illusion that he'll be keen on rescheduling. This is too much drama for any sane person to want to deal with.

"I should go." I try to smile, but it feels more like a grimace.

"Can I walk you to your room?" he asks, surprising me.

I shake my head. "You don't have to."

He gently takes my hand in his. "I want to."

He keeps my hand in his as we go to the elevators and toward my room. We are silent the whole time, but it's not awkward. It's comforting. When we finally reach my door, I place my hand on the knob and turn to face him.

My breath catches as I look up at Chase. He is, without a doubt, the most attractive man I have ever seen. He's tall—easily six inches above me—and his broad shoulders fill out his sweatshirt effortlessly. His dark hair is slightly tousled, like he's run his hands through it a few times, giving him a rugged, natural look. His jawline is sharp, with a faint trace of stubble that adds to the raw appeal of his face. His eyes are a striking shade of blue. He's dressed casually, yet his outfit somehow makes him seem even more magnetic. A fitted black hoodie with the New York Devils logo sits perfectly on his frame, hugging his shoulders and chest, and the sleeves are pushed up slightly, showing off his forearms. His jeans are a faded, well-worn blue, fitting him just right, and his sneakers are simple, but they somehow seem to match his effortless style. There's nothing flashy about his clothes, but on him, everything feels just...right.

"I'm sorry about tonight," I finally say, my voice trembling slightly as my chest rises and falls rapidly.

I can see Chase struggling to decide where to look. He leans forward, and I feel his breath in my ear.

"You have nothing to be sorry for." He takes a breath and gives me a soft kiss on the cheek before pulling back and whispering, "Plus, now I have your room number."

I laugh, tilting my head back while pressed between the door and Chase. "You're a sneaky one."

He remains close, his breath warm against my skin. "I really want to kiss you," he whispers, his voice low, sending a shiver through me, leaving me breathless and trembling. "But I know tonight isn't the night. When I kiss you for the first time, I want it to be a great day, and I know today's not that day. But I couldn't leave without at least telling you how badly I want to kiss you."

I turn my head slightly to meet his gaze. I desperately want to tell him I feel the same, but I've never had a man talk to me like this. With emotion and lust, it's sending me into shock, so instead of saying "Me too," I smile softly and turn away.

As soon as the door closes behind me, my back falls into the door, and a sob escapes my lips. My arm flies over my face to muffle my cries, but it's pointless. The floodgates are open and I'm a mess. Not even bothering to change, I fling myself into bed, continuing to cry.

Fucking Campbell.

When he showed up at the bar, I thought I could talk him down, get him out of there, and still enjoy my night with Chase, but that was short-lived. Campbell made it clear as soon as he started talking that he wasn't going to make a divorce easy. I knew he wouldn't react well when he was served with papers, but showing up at the hotel and making a scene isn't his style, and a part of me feels guilty for putting him through this. For all his faults, Campbell was thrown into the same life I was and we became products of our environment.

On paper, we should fit, but we just don't.

Desperate to stop crying, I reach for my mom's journal, opening the last entry I had earmarked with a gum wrapper.

April 3, 1992

Daniel was so happy. I think we may have made another baby...

I quickly flip the page to the next entry because, *ew*, it's still my parents.

April 10, 1992

It was my first doctor's appointment, and it was confirmed I was 14 weeks pregnant, just getting into the second trimester. They said the nonstop nausea is normal, and it should be easing up soon. But I won't lie, it feels never-ending. But it's okay, I won't complain.

I flip again, coming across pages of scribbles but no actual words. The next entry is four months later.

August 19, 1992

I will love her.

I will love her.

I will love her.

I repeat it all day long, and it's taken me four months to even write it down.

I HATE pregnancy. There, I said it.

I know, I know, it's supposed to be this incredible journey, and trust me, I am impressed with what my body is doing, but I hate it. I hate how I feel. I hate being touched. We haven't had sex in months, and I know Daniel hates it. I do too, but I hate the idea of being touched even more.

10 more weeks.

November 26, 1992

WE HAVE A BABY FOR THANKSGIVING! Abigail Gene Keenan was born on November 16th, 1992. She weighed 6lbs 7oz and was 16 inches long. She is the perfect angel and already has Daniel wrapped around his finger.

Have to eat pie now!

I close the journal. I like ending the night with passages where my mother seems happy. As more tears stream down my cheeks, I wipe them away.

"Do I sleep or eat?" I mutter, my voice hoarse from the lump in my throat.

Sitting up in bed, I know sleep is a long shot. The gnawing hunger in my stomach makes sure of that. With a groan, I roll over, reaching for the phone on the night-stand to call room service. Just as my fingers graze the receiver, two quick knocks echo from the door, followed by the hurried sound of footsteps retreating down the hallway.

I freeze, heart thudding, before climbing out of bed. The plush hotel robe swishes around my legs as I tiptoe to the door, rising onto my toes to peek through the peephole. Through the distorted fisheye lens, I spot the gleaming silhouette of a bar cart just outside. My curiosity spikes as I lean back and open the door, the cool hallway air brushing against my flushed cheeks exposing a cart filled with over ten dishes with silver tin covers, two martini shakers, a bowl of olives, and a small white envelope with my name written on the top with a gray marker. My heart begins to race as my hand reaches for the envelope. I flip it over and pull the small hotel stationery out of the envelope.

One of everything I've seen you order before. If nothing else, the triple-fudge chocolate brownie will make you smile.
– Chase

A grin tugs at my lips, despite the tears that threaten to spill again. My hand lingers over one of the lids, and when I lift it, it reveals a steak and truffle potatoes—the first meal we ate together. I unveil another and see the French onion soup that I get every day for lunch. Another reveals a Caesar salad with extra cheese, and my stomach growls at the sight. I pull the cart into my room. Once the door is behind and the cart is secured, I pick up the shaker to find it full of prepared dirty martinis. I pour it into my glass and take a sip, then release a big sigh.

For the first time in hours, I feel a flicker of warmth, a sense of being cared for in a way that doesn't demand anything in return. My fingers drift to the smallest dish on the cart, and as I lift its cover, I find the brownie he mentioned—gooey, decadent, and topped with a generous fudge drizzle.

"Fucking Chase," I whisper under my breath, his name feeling strangely intimate in the quiet of my suite.

A smile breaks fully across my face as I grab my phone and type a text before taking another massive sip of my martini and diving into all the food before me.

Me: *You are amazing. Thank you.*

CHAPTER EIGHT

Avery

Waking up the next morning feels like a blend of being run over by a truck and having eaten every single bite from a late-night food cart. Despite the throbbing ache and lingering exhaustion, I have to focus on the job interview ahead. I have been separating my personal feelings from my professional responsibilities my whole life, and today's no different.

The challenge, however, is that this interview is uncomfortably intertwined with my personal life. I'm interviewing for a position with the New York City Devils for their preseason charity series—Chase's team. This charity campaign is impressive, investing over $500,000 annually to make these events happen and raising over a million each year. It's a fantastic career opportunity, and I'm confident I have a strong idea that could secure the job. Still, after last night, it feels strange going into this interview without Chase knowing, especially since he didn't respond to my text last night.

I arrive at the arena thirty minutes early, giving myself some extra time to admire the building. I never went to professional sports events as a kid, so now, every time I visit an arena I can't help but be in awe.

"Do you need some help?" a deep, masculine voice pulls me from my reverie.

I turn to see three guys in Devils sweatshirts standing nearby, making me laugh nervously. They must be players. The first one is tall, probably around six-foot-three, with broad shoulders that fill out his sweatshirt impressively. His dark hair is tousled in a way that makes him look effortlessly cool, and his eyes, a sharp shade of blue, are fixed on me with a playful glint. He grins, revealing a set of straight teeth, but there's something intimidating about how he carries himself, as if he's used to commanding attention without even trying.

The second guy is stockier, but with a surprising athleticism in his build. His hair is shorter, buzzed close to his scalp, and his thick arms are visible even under the oversized sweatshirt. His hazel eyes are warm but calculating, as if he's measuring me up while trying to hide the curiosity behind a cocky smirk. There's a scar above his eyebrow that adds a touch of ruggedness to his otherwise boyish face.

The third guy is leaner, with an angular jaw and a confident posture that suggests he's always one step ahead. His dark brown hair is styled in a way that looks meticulously messy, and his green eyes flicker with amusement.

He stands slightly apart from the others, but his presence is no less commanding. There's a certain charm to him, but it's the kind that could easily go from teasing to serious, depending on his mood.

I smile awkwardly, trying to hide that I'm suddenly very aware of how out of place I feel in front of these guys. "Oh no, sorry," I say, still slightly flustered. "I have an interview soon and was just taking in the arena. It's beautiful."

"It is," the same guy replies with a friendly smile. "Do you need help finding your way around?"

My eyes glance between them all. "Umm..." I hesitate. I could use help—I am directionally challenged at best, and getting to know the players will only help when I am planning the events.

"Yeah, that would be nice. I'm Avery." I extend a hand, and he grabs it to shake.

"Riley," he replies with a warm smile. "These are my teammates, James and Billy." He gestures to the other two guys, who both nod in greeting.

"Hi, guys," I say, offering a smile.

As we walk toward the elevators, Riley leads the conversation. We quickly fall into a comfortable rhythm, and by the time we reach the elevators, it feels like we're old friends, making the nerves I had earlier seem to fade into the background.

"So you're here for the event planning position, I'm guessing?" James asks.

I nod my head. "Yeah. I had a pre-interview already and sent them my plan last night. Your general manager, Neil, already said he loved it, but it's between me and another person," I say, getting excited about the presentation and proving we can make these events come to life.

"You'll get it," Billy says, leaning his head back and closing his eyes.

My eyes widen and I look at Riley and James. "Oh my god, he talked to me," I tease, and I hear Billy laugh.

"Oh my god, he laughs," James says. "Now we need to make sure you get the job."

"We should grab lunch after your interview, and you can meet my wife. She loves helping with our charity events, and she'll make sure to rope all the WAG ladies together."

"Well, I would love to meet your wife. She seems lovely, but we are jumping the gun a little. We don't know if I'm going to get the job."

"You'll get it," they all say in unison, and I laugh, shaking my head. "You Devils players."

"You know more of us?" James gives me a teasing pouty face. "But we were going to be the players to bring you in. Who do you know? Are they rookies?"

I laugh again, and the elevator dings on the floor. "Don't worry. You three are my favorite. I know another player because we live in the same hotel."

All three guys come to a halt and stare at me wide-eyed. "You know Chase?"

"Uhh..." I hesitate. "Yes," I say slowly.

They stare for another second longer. "You're 'mystery girl'?" Billy asks in a slow, monotone voice.

They continue to stare until all three of them start laughing uncontrollably.

"You guys," I whine. "What? Is he a scumbag or something? This is not good for my nerves before the interview."

Riley pulls himself together, walks up to me, places
his hands on my shoulders, and leans forward to look
me in the eyes. "Chase is one of the best guys I know,
and we already told you you're getting the job. We're just
happy we got to meet you without Chase around first."
His smile is earnest, and I don't know why I trust these
three random players I met five minutes ago, but I do.

James walks up. "That was sweet, really, but before you
go in there and kill it, we need a quick picture with all of
us."

I don't have time to question it before the three of
them surround me with the biggest, cheesiest smiles on
their faces, and James is holding his phone in front of us
to take a selfie. I give an awkward half-smile and then see
Neil walking toward us.

I quickly push past the guys and walk toward Neil.
"Good morning, sir. It's great to meet you in person." I
put my hand out and he shakes it.

"It's great to meet you as well," he replies with a wel-
coming smile. "These guys giving you any trouble?" he
asks, looking at Riley, James, and Billy.

The three of them take a few steps toward us as I say,
"No, sir. They were kind enough to help me find it up
here."

"Neil." They nod.

"Gentleman, shouldn't you be doing some conditioning
downstairs?

"Yep," James answers quickly.

"So why are you not down there?"

"We just wanted to see if we are right and you're going to hire her?"

He looks at me and then back at them when Riley says, "It's true. We're pretty positive you're going to."

"And why is that?" Neil asks curiously, and I close my eyes in embarrassment.

What the hell is happening right now?

"You loved her proposal?" Riley asks.

Oh. My. God. They are telling him about his email. What if he takes that the wrong way? I should have never said anything to three strangers in a stupid elevator.

"And?"

"I don't think you've ever said you've loved a proposal before it was presented in your entire life. In fact, I know you haven't. Last season, you harped on how the presentation is key to seeing how a charity event will come to life for forty-five minutes," Riley responds before James interjects, "Argo, she got the job."

The three of them walk back toward the elevators. My jaw goes slack, and my mouth hangs open in shock. I look back at Neil, who is laughing at the guys.

"I'm so sorry. I literally just met them," I say, still in awe of the last ten minutes.

***

Once I finally managed to close my jaw and we walked into the conference room, I delivered my presentation and went through the three events:

1. The Annual Youth Hockey Clinic: In the morning and early afternoon, Devils players will work with local kids, teaching them the basics of hockey and providing guidance. To elevate the event, we'll add a charity game in the evening. We'll invite another NHL team we are friendly with to participate, and all ticket and concession proceeds will be split between our charity and theirs. Additionally, we'll feature the kids who participated in the clinic earlier in the day on the ice at the start of the game for a fantastic PR opportunity.

2. The Charity Tailgate: my creation, meticulously planned from scratch. We'll host a carnival featuring all our professional sports teams. Athletes will engage in various games and activities, including a flag football game and beer Olympics, in an adults-only tent. A dedicated children's area will ensure a family-friendly atmosphere where fans can meet their favorite hockey and football players. We will also have performers and a tent selling signed jerseys. The jerseys should help us with our total donations by a considerable margin.

3. The Charity Gala and Auction—this is also a yearly event that the Devils do, but the auction will be a new addition. I've proposed making it the

final charity event of the preseason, using it to celebrate and honor the players. We'll conclude with an award ceremony where each player will be presented a trophy and a toast by a loved one. Neil fully supports this idea but wants to keep it a surprise for the players. I love the idea, so it's good I will meet Riley's wife; she should be able to help me coordinate that.

I lay it out clearly at the end of the presentation: Last year, they raised $500,000 for charity after expenses. I'm projecting $1 million with my events, and I'm happy to say the guys were right. I killed it, and Neil hires me on the spot. Now, I just need to make these events a success and tell Chase that he will be seeing a lot of me over the next couple of weeks.

After we go over some initial logistics, I tell Neil I will start securing some vendors and will be in touch with the next steps soon. We say our goodbyes, and as soon as I am out of his vicinity, my mind snaps back to Chase and the other players I met. Riley said Chase is one of the best guys he knows, so I assume they're close. But does that mean Chase already knows I'm here?

My suspicions are confirmed when the elevator doors open to reveal a flushed, sweaty, and shirtless Chase, with Riley, James, and Billy all laughing behind him.

CHAPTER NINE

Chase

I'm halfway through my workout, sweat dripping down my brow as I push through the last set of deadlifts, when Riley, James, and Billy stroll into the gym. Their laughter echoes off the walls, and I immediately know they're up to something.

"Nice of you to finally show up," I say, setting the bar down and glancing at them. "Where've you guys been?"

"Helping someone find their way to the conference rooms for an interview," Billy replies, grinning like he just won the lottery.

"So all three of you went? That's a bit overkill, don't you think?"

Riley smirks. "She was cool. We're grabbing lunch with her after her interview. Neil's going to hire her anyway."

"You're grabbing lunch with someone you just met...who might work with us?" I ask slowly, trying to piece this together.

I look at Riley, hoping for some clarity, but he just shrugs. "Jemmeye's already on her way. I want to introduce her so she can help with the charity events."

"But she hasn't even been hired yet," I point out, my brow furrowing.

They exchange a look before answering in unison. "She's going to get it."

I move to another machine, shaking my head as I continue my workout. Meanwhile, the guys linger around like they're here for a social hour instead of a workout.

"Do you want to join us for lunch? Neil says they're almost done with the interview," Riley says as he stares at his phone, focused.

I glance at him, then back to the weights. "Nah, I'm actually working out—unlike you guys. I've got another hour to go."

"Are you sure?" Riley presses. "You don't want to meet her? We'll be working closely with her for the rest of the preseason."

"I'll meet her next time," I reply evenly, not wanting to be dragged into whatever they're scheming.

James steps closer, a teasing grin on his face as he pulls out his phone. "Come on, man, don't you at least want to see her? She's hot."

He holds up the screen, and the image sends a jolt through my chest. There they are—James, Riley, and Billy—grinning like idiots with *Avery*.

I take a step back. "What the hell? Why do you have a picture with Avery?"

Their laughter explodes, loud and obnoxious, as if they've been waiting for this exact reaction.

My chest constricts in a way I've never felt before. After I left Avery's room door, I heard her cry, and I swear my heart shattered. It took everything in me not to break the door and scoop her into my arms. Instead, I walked back down to the bar, talked to Steven, and ordered one of every entrée she has ordered since she's been staying at the Four Seasons.

I wrote a quick note and left it with the bar cart, knocked on her door, and sprinted to the staircase. I didn't want to force her to see anybody if she wanted to be alone. When she texted me, I wanted to text her back, but also wanted to give her space. But now she's here, and she didn't tell me, and maybe I should have texted her back.

Riley must see my feelings written on my face because he hits the guys, and they all stop laughing. "We really did meet her and show her where to go, and then you got brought up, and we realized she's your hotel mystery girl. You know we had to mess with you." His voice is sincere as he throws an arm over my shoulder. "Now she's currently heading down the elevator," he says, flashing his phone, which shows a text from Neil.

> **Neil:** We hired Avery. Get ready. You're about to be busy as hell.

"Is it our faces you want her to see or yours when she gets to the main floor?" he asks, and something clicks in my brain. I need to see her. My legs sprint toward the elevators, and I hear the guys quickly following behind. I reach the elevators just as the bell dings, signaling their arrival. When the doors open, it's Avery, ready to bring me to my knees.

"Hi." Her voice is soft.

Our eyes meet, and I take her in—you would never be able to tell she sobbed herself to sleep last night. My fingers itch to reach out to her.

"We told you you'd get the job," James cheers, and I glance back at the guys, all grinning like idiots.

She shakes her head, smiling, and a grin spreads across my face. I love seeing her smile.

"Congratulations," I say, gripping her elbow with a firm, reassuring squeeze.

"Thanks," she replies, placing her hand over mine and giving it a gentle squeeze back.

"All right, let's head to lunch. Jemmeye just got to the place we're going next door," Riley announces.

"Oh, you guys were serious?" Avery asks.

"Of course we were serious. Let's go see my sissy-in-law," James says, wrapping an arm around Avery and kissing her cheek as they approach the door.

My fists clench instinctively. I'm not a violent guy by nature, but seeing James kiss Avery's cheek makes me want to rip my best friend's throat out.

Billy steps up behind me and slaps a hand on my shoulder. "Want to join us for lunch now?"

★★★

Lunch is great. Avery fits in so effortlessly, it's as if she's known everyone for years rather than fifteen minutes. She and Jemmeye hit it off immediately, chattering non-stop through the entire meal. By the time dessert arrives, they've already made plans for a night out this weekend, and Jemmeye has eagerly volunteered to help with the charity events, rallying the wives and girlfriends to get involved.

James, on the other hand, practically shoved me out of the way to claim the seat beside her during lunch. I had half a mind to follow through on my earlier threat of ripping my best friend's throat out, but then I realized—maybe sitting directly across from her is the better move.

It gives me a perfect vantage point, and I take full advantage, sliding my legs out under the table. Every so often, I "accidentally" bump into hers, especially whenever James tries to monopolize her attention. Each time, she glances my way with a small smile, her eyes sparkling with amusement as she rolls them dramatically. But every now and again, she moves her leg just enough to press against mine.

On the walk back to the hotel, Avery tells me her version of meeting the guys, her interview, and the whole charity plan. It honestly sounds incredible. Her goal of raising $1 million is ambitious, but I have no doubt she can pull it off.

"You're amazing, you know that?" I say at one point, which she brushes off with a shy smile. I don't think she gets praise very much, and it only makes me want to give her more of it.

When we reach her floor, it's barely past 1 p.m., but I'm not about to let her go without walking her to her door.

"So why didn't you tell me?" I finally ask as we stroll down the hallway.

"I wanted to," she says, stopping to look at me.

I stop, locking eyes with her. She places a hand on my bicep, and I feel a rush of warmth spread across my body.

"With everything last night, it just didn't seem like the time, and I didn't know how you'd feel about me going for a job where we'll be working together closely for a few months."

"Hey," I say, placing a finger under her chin and tilting it up to get a better view of her face. "Any time I get to spend with you, working or otherwise, makes me nothing but ecstatic. I know we haven't known each other long, Avery, but I think you're one of my favorite people already."

Her hand squeezes my arm, and my hand instinctively finds her hip, pulling her a step closer to me. I feel my heart rate increase, and my breath becomes more ragged.

"I think you're one of my favorite people too." Her voice is barely a whisper, but it's loud enough for me to hear, and I love every word of it.

"I'm going to kiss you, Avery."

"Uh," she stutters, shuffling with nerves. "I don't know if we should—"

I place my fingers across her lips to stop her from finishing that sentence. I'm sure it's filled with logic and reason, but standing in front of Avery, I don't give two fucks about logic or reason.

"If you don't want me to kiss you because you're not ready or you're not into me, then I will back away. But if you feel even a fraction of what I'm feeling right now, don't let being afraid stop you. Today's a good day." It's my voice that's almost a whisper now. My face is now only centimeters from her face. My eyes locked with hers, waiting for any signal of which way she was leaning. Then she smiles, places her hands around my neck and pulls me into her.

The second my lips connect with hers, I'm a goner. The way her lips move on mine and her body molds into me. It has never felt like this. I take two steps, pushing her back into the door, not daring to take my lips off hers. My hands are moving in a frenzy, desperate to touch every part of her, and I feel my dick growing harder by the second.

She pulls back from the kiss slightly, and I jolt back, worried she's changed her mind.

"Are you okay? Do you want to stop?" My voice is urgent, terrified I just scared her off.

She smiles, her face is flushed, lips swollen from our kiss, and my dick twitches at the sight of her. "Not a chance, but I do think we should go into the room," her voice teases as she looks at her room.

I have conveniently backed us up into her room door. I nod eagerly. "Yes."

She laughs as she holds the key up to her door, the sound of the lock turning echoes before she opens the door, and I follow her in. When the door closes behind me, Avery whips around and pushes me into the door, and I am stunned in the best way possible.

My hands fly to her hips, pulling her into me as closely as possible. Now that we're in the room, I don't plan on letting her go. I lift her and her legs wrap around my waist. I walk her through the hallway toward the bed. My lips reluctantly pull from hers.

"If you want to stop, just say so, okay, honey?"

I want this. Bad. But I know that where she is at is complicated. I search her eyes looking for any sign that she doesn't want this. "This is a terrible idea, but I don't want you to stop. Please don't stop." Her voice is pleading, and I drop her into the bed.

"Good girl." I smirk, letting my lips tease hers until I can't see straight, and then I lean in and press my mouth against hers, letting our tongues tangle, and I can't get enough.

God, I'm going to enjoy this.

My hands find the buttons of her pants, and as I undo them, she's reaching, trying to pull up my sweater that's now half tangled in one arm, and her pants are looking about the same.

We both pause, letting out a small laugh.

I pull the rest of my sweater over my head and lean back into her lips. "Getting impatient, beautiful?"

She nods, and I slowly pull down her black panties feeling a jolt of pleasure zip right to my dick, which is now unbearably hard against her thigh. My other travels up her stomach, I pull her bra to the side, rubbing my thumb over her nipples, straining to come free. I pinch her nipple, teasing her, drawing a breathy noise from her mouth.

I'm so hard, I feel like a sixteen-year-old kid about to cum his pants. My breath becomes ragged as my hand leaves her breast and travels back down her stomach, her skin exploding with goose bumps everywhere I touch.

My hand slides lower, dipping into her panties, and as soon as my fingers graze her folds I feel her and she's soaked. And then I do what I've been dying to do since I saw her for the first time. Drop to my damn knees.

My head dips as I give her light kisses between her thighs. Her skin is soft like silk, and my tongue and dick love it as I lick my way up to her clit. I have the primal need to growl *"mine"* into her pussy, but, with the full knowledge it'll probably freak her out, I keep my mouth shut and give her what she wants. Long licks and gentle sucking until she's squirming beneath me.

The first time hooking up with someone can be weird sometimes, you're getting to know each other's likes and dislikes—what makes them tick. But with Avery, it doesn't feel weird at all. Her body is responding so well, I can feel every pulse against my tongue, and if I'm right, she's close.

I slowly thrust two fingers into her, and I continue licking her. Her body is vibrating and I don't intend on stopping until she's a withering mess underneath me. My fingers are plunging in and out of her, my thumb doing circles around her clit.

"Chase, oh my god," she moans, grabbing two fistfuls of my hair. She's damn near trembling. I plant one hand on her hip, digging my fingers into her creamy flesh. I pull out my two fingers and suck her nice and long before entering her core again.

"You're doing so good for me, baby, look how perfect you look," I praise her, and I feel her start to fall apart. One finger in and out, two fingers in and out, and then as soon as I pull them out, I plunge all three in, and it sends my girl right over the edge.

Trembling, soaked, and my name coming out of her mouth, I ride out her orgasm, all while knowing there's no turning back.

I want this girl.

***

I walk out of the bathroom, flop onto the bed, and watch as Avery walks over to the bed. Her hair is a perfect mess, and the white plush hotel robe is wrapped around her. Her hand finds her hair and she adjusts it.

"You made me a mess." She laughs as she plops onto the bed and hands me her water bottle. I wrap my hand around the bottle, but instead of taking it, I use it to lean forward, kissing her lips. They're cold from the water she just drank, but it sends a jolt of electricity through my body. *Fuck, what is that?*

She softly groans and then places a hand on my chest and pulls away. "We should talk." Her voice a sadder tone than a moment ago.

"No way, are you going to hit me with a 'we should talk' right after we hooked up, mystery girl? Plus"—I shake my head—"you don't want me to feel like a cheap date. What am I, just a piece of meat?" I fold my arms back behind my head, flexing my muscles.

She laughs and throws my shirt at me.

"I'm being serious, Chase." She's still smiling, but I can tell I won't be in a minute.

I pull my shirt over my head and slip my arms into the sleeves. Sitting up, I swing one leg over the edge of the bed and place my foot on the floor to steady myself.

"Serious," I repeat, mocking a faux-serious gesture, gaining another laugh from her.

"We are about to work together for at least six weeks, but realistically more like ten," she starts.

"Correct."

"We live in the same hotel."

"My favorite perk," I add.

"And I am still married."

"You filed for divorce. While I will say you clearly had terrible taste, I won't hold it against you."

I know she is trying to talk herself out of this, not me.

"I filed, but he hasn't signed, and nothing has happened..." She pauses and takes a breath. "And he's made it very clear that he's going to string this out for as long as possible."

My fists clench. "I'm going to kill him," I mutter.

She scoffs. "Yeah, get in line." She pauses again, taking another deep breath. "I like you, Chase. But I'm not like you," she continues, her eyes searching mine for understanding. "I can't blend work and personal. Right now, every part of my life is tangled together in one big spaghetti pot, and I can't handle it. I'm not stable enough. I need to get through this divorce without any extra complications. If I start dating someone now, Campbell will wage an all-out war."

My jaw tightens at the mention of her ex, but I force myself to stay calm. "I'm not afraid of your dickhead ex, and you shouldn't be either."

She lets out a frustrated laugh. "Fine. Take Campbell out of the equation. We'll still be working together for at least the next two months. That's another complication."

"Exactly," I counter, leaning just a bit closer. "Only two months."

She stares at me, her eyes pleading, and I can see it—she needs me to give in. So I do it—for her.

"Fine," I relent, my voice dropping. "We'll be friends while we work together. That gives you time to figure things out with Campbell. Once the season starts, we'll talk again about this."

She exhales sharply, her shoulders sagging slightly as relief washes over her face, mixed with something I can't quite place.

"Plus," I add, smirking, "I bet you won't make it past week five."

Her head tips back as she laughs, the sound filling the space between us. "You don't think I can resist you?" she teases, pointing at me and giving me a once-over. "You're good, Chase. But you're not that good."

I lean forward, letting the challenge light up my face. "All right, mystery girl. You think so?" My eyebrow quirks, daring her. "Let's make this interesting—a bet."

Her laughter fades into a curious smile, her gaze narrowing. "What's the bet?"

I let the idea marinate for a moment before it clicks. "Who caves and gives in first? I bet you won't last until the charity gala. You want me, Avs. You'll be begging for my fingers to be inside soon enough."

"Easy," she fires back without hesitation, tilting her head. "But what stops *you* from giving in first? Since, you know, you obviously want me just as much." Her tone is light, teasing, but her eyes glint with the same challenge.

I tap my fingers against my chin, pretending to think. "What do you want if I lose?"

She hums, a mischievous smile curling her lips. "You'll donate the difference so I meet our charity goal *before* the gala. I want the gala to be the cherry on top."

"Ooh, betting my money? You think that'll make me hold out longer?" I chuckle, shaking my head. "You don't know me at all."

She laughs with me, and I know she thinks I'm joking. What she doesn't know is I'd happily write that check right now. But I'll hold strong these next couple of months because I know she needs that.

"And if you cave?" I ask, my voice dropping as I place my hand just a little closer to hers.

She rolls her eyes dramatically. "What do you want?"

A grin spreads across my face, broad and unapologetic. "That's easy. *You*."

Her cheeks flush, and for a moment, the playful bravado slips as something softer flickers in her eyes. Then she smirks and holds out her hand. "Deal."

I shake her hand, holding on for a beat longer than necessary, my thumb brushing against hers. "Game on, mystery girl."

Her laughter follows me as I walk away, and for the first time in a while I feel like I've already won.

Chapter Ten

Avery

Let's talk about the last three weeks of my life.

My mother died, and I made an ass out of myself at her funeral so my siblings haven't talked to me since.

I left my husband in the middle of the night, filed for divorce, and am now living in a hotel.

I met an incredibly hot NHL player and easily had the best orgasm of my life, and now I am planning charity events for his team. Oh, and we decided to be "just friends."

Do I know how to blow up my life or what?

I stare at my computer. I've been sitting at the desk in my hotel room for the last seven hours, mapping out every meticulous detail of the first charity event. The hockey clinic is an annual event, and the signups, set up before I was hired, sold out quickly—great news and an easy win. With fifty children paying for admission and us sponsoring another fifty children, we've netted about $5,000 so far.

Historically, they've made an additional $5,000 from food sales and another $5,000 from merchandise. I'm projecting we'll double those numbers this year. I've added five new food options, all from volunteers who are donating their profits in exchange for marketing exposure with the New York Devils and support for a good cause.

My major challenge is the charity game. I figured it would be straightforward: invite the nearest NHL team to participate and let them take 50 percent of the donations. Simple, right? It should be an easy yes. Yeah, no. Apparently, the Devils have rivalries up and down the East Coast, and none are willing to set their differences aside for charity this close to the season. It's ridiculous, but I'm too busy and too screwed to worry about that right now.

I groan and push away from my desk, pacing back and forth. "What do they want? What do they want?" I mutter to myself.

New York Devils fans want—*and there it is.*

"Yes!" I squeal. The idea. Why I didn't think about this before is beyond me. Without wasting another moment, I plop back into my chair and draft an email to Neil.

To: Neil Declan
From: Avery Keenan
Subject: Retired Player Roster
Hi Neil,

Happy Tuesday! Could you please send me the names, emails, phone numbers, and addresses of all retired NY Devils players in good standing? Ideally, those who retired in the last ten years. I have an exciting idea!

Thanks so much!

To: Avery Keenan

From: Neil Declan

Subject: Re: Retired Player Roster

Avery—See attached! Let's meet tomorrow to discuss the next steps. Looking forward to it!

Best,

Neil

★★★

I figure I need to get at least ten to twelve of these guys to say yes. I review Neil's list. There are over twenty-five names—plenty to choose from. Should I invite them all? Who are the fan favorites? Who will draw the biggest crowd?

I let out another frustrated groan, not knowing if I can handle any more time in front of my computer today. But if I'm meeting Neil tomorrow, I need to get moving on this. My hand hovers over my phone, knowing Chase would be able to help, but the idea of seeing Chase not even twenty-four hours after we hooked up has my body temperature rising. I don't want to know what will happen if I'm alone with him. Well, I do. But I can't, because, unfortunately, everything I told him last night was true.

We are working together. I am getting a divorce. It's all just messy, and now our little bet—it's thrilling and terrifying, and I haven't entirely sorted that out yet, but I do know I want to win, which means not caving.

I wish I could say that as a twenty-eight-year-old woman, I know how to be friends with a man whom I am attracted to, but with Chase I just don't see how it's possible. So I take an approach to getting my job done, see Chase, and have plenty of chaperons.

Group Name: Help Avs & NY Devils
Riley, James, Billy, Jemmeye, Chase

Me: *SOS. Avery is buying dinner for all included in this group chat.*

Me: Four Seasons Bar
One Hour
Required gossip topic: Retired NY Devils
Players

Chase: What? How do you have everyone's numbers?

Jemmeye: OMG. YES. Riley and I are on the way now…I can tell you the hottest ones.

Billy: Is attractiveness a factor in this gossip?

Avery: Of course.

Chase: Avery—why are you inviting them? I'll just come to your room and tell you everything you need to know *winky face*

Jemmeye: Eww. Chase. No. We are already on the way. I know you said an hour, but we'll be there in 30.

Billy: Okay, I'm coming. Where's James? He's a statistics wiz, so he'd probably be helpful if we are actually talking players.

James: I'm just leaving the gym. I'm coming. Avs—can I take a shower in your room? *winky face*

Chase: No.

Chase: You can shower in my room.

I throw my head back laughing before replying and heading to the bar to wait for them.

***

As soon as I exit the elevators and head to the bar, Cedric follows me from the front desk. "Avery," he huffs when he finally reaches me.

"Hey," I say. "Are you okay? What's up?"

"Yeah, listen—" he starts, then looks around to make sure no one is around. "When you checked in, we booked for three weeks. That three weeks is running out, so I was going to auto-rebook you another three weeks…" He pauses like he's not sure what to say next. Does he not think I want him to update my booking? I am about to speak when he starts again. "When I went, it said that the credit card on file was no longer active. I called the bank because sometimes we have system issues, and it seems that the card was canceled. You're good until Friday, but I will need a new card by tomorrow if you want to rebook."

"Campbell," I mutter. He said he would make it difficult, but I didn't think he'd try to cancel my credit cards. It's a useless step—we've always kept our money separate, and our prenup is going to ensure an equal split, so canceling my cards just because we share the same last name and are still married…it's unnecessary and petty. It is purely to waste my time and make my life harder, which drives me insane. I fight the urge to head to my old apartment and give Campbell a piece of my mind, but I know that's what he wants. He wants my reaction, and I won't give him the satisfaction.

I take a breath and look at Cedric, giving the biggest, fakest smile I can muster. "I will bring a new card down in the morning. Sorry about the trouble."

He reciprocates and squeezes my arm before shuffling back to his desk. I know I should text my sister for help. She could help get this divorce done and over with, but we've never been close, and I don't know how to ask her for help. She should know I'm going through a divorce and be offering to help, but as far as she knows, I left our mother's funeral and went on with my life like normal.

I continue walking toward the bar, getting my head back into work mode. I printed the list Neil sent me and plan to go through it and get everyone's opinions on who should be my priority when trying to contact them to come to play at the charity again.

Retired Devils legends vs. current-day Devils.

In this city? This will sell. I can sell this game. Now it's just a matter of who will have the best draw and make it the best game.

My eyes scan the room and land on Chase, sitting alone at the only large table in the corner that seats six. When he notices me, a grin spreads across his face, and I'm suddenly transported back to last night, remembering his head between my legs. I don't realize I'm frozen in place until I see Chase stand up and walk toward me.

"Well, hello there, beautiful," he says, his voice overly enthusiastic.

"Chase. Hi," I respond, forcing a smile as I move toward the table.

"Are you sure you can handle sitting alone with me? Our chaperones aren't here yet."

He plops down across from me, his legs intentionally brushing mine under the table. I glare at him, knowing he's doing this on purpose.

"No chaperones, just a need for friends and NY Devils insights. The more opinions, the better," I reply, hoping my excuse sounds believable.

"Mm-hmm," he hums, his leg continuing to nudge mine. "No harm in caving now, Avs. You've lasted twen-

ty-four hours. That's twenty hours longer than I expected."

I glare at him, ready to retort, but before I can, our four
friends walk through the door and head toward us.

I jump up and wrap my arms around Jemmeye in a hug.
As my face nears her ear, I whisper urgently, "Don't let me
sit next to or across from Chase." I pull back and give her
pleading eyes.

She nods, understanding immediately.

I hug the rest of the group, and Jemmeye directs everyone where she wants them to sit. Our rectangular table
soon has Jemmeye, James, and me on one side and Riley,
Billy, and Chase across from us.

Chase could only mess with me now if he crosses over
with James or Billy. As we take our seats, I give Chase a
wink. He just smiles, shaking his head.

"All right, so here's the deal," I start. "After the hockey
clinic this year, we're doing a charity game. I was thinking
the Devils versus a surrounding state NHL team, but it
seems that you guys have a rivalry with almost every
team near us." I let the accusation hang in the air.

"Yeah. Because we're better," Billy says matter-of-factly, causing the other guys to join in.

Jemmeye and I look at each other and roll our eyes.

"Anyway," I continue, trying to refocus the conversation, "now I'm thinking of a game between current and
retired players from the last ten years."

"Oh, that's sick," Riley says, clearly excited.

"Right? I'm aiming for ten or twelve max. I need to know
who would be the best draws. Who should I contact first?"

"Aren't you from around here?" James asks from his seat next to mine.

"Yeah, but I don't know much about hockey," I admit, recalling how I told Chase the same thing. My eyes instinctively seek him out, and when they land on him, he's already watching me with a soft smile. I resist the urge to get up and kiss him, realizing I'm more grateful than ever for the friends between us.

***

After an hour I have my list, and the guys did most of the work for me, calling retired players they know and asking them to participate. We have already nailed down eight, with three maybes.

I make sure to say goodbye to everyone before Chase and rush to my room. If I had stayed, he would have walked me to my room, and I don't trust myself not to pull him in and have a repeat of last night.

Once I'm in bed, my mind starts to wander. Should I call Abigail? I glance at my mother's journals, which I've been avoiding but now feel compelled to read.

I pick up the journal I was reading earlier, flipping to the last passage I was on.

December 16, 1992

She's beautiful, my sweet Abigail, and I love her more than I could have imagined, but I've never wanted to sleep more in my life. The doctors say it's colic, but it feels like I'm losing my grip. Daniel's back at work, and I can barely remember the last time I spoke to anyone. My friends and family seem like distant memories now. It's just her and me, and sometimes, it feels like I'm alone in this.

I love her. I do. But I just need a moment to breathe.

December 26th, 1992

The holidays are over, and honestly, I'm relieved. It was harder than I thought it would be—everyone talking, drinking, eating, and I'm sitting there, trying to pretend I'm fine while everyone stares at my plate and judges the way I'm feeding my baby. It's so frustrating watching them devour everything I want but can't have. Abigail's reflux is impossible unless I live on crackers and dry toast.

At least there's one small victory: I'm back to my pre-baby weight. But that feels hollow. Who cares about that when I'm barely holding it together? But it's all I have.

January 1st, 1993

I'm telling myself I'll write more in '93. I need to. I promised myself I would pull out of this funk and remember who I was before everything changed. I will find my way back, even if it feels impossible some days. I need to be the person I was—the one who dreamed and laughed and lived without so much weight on her shoulders.

The good news: Abigail is sleeping more than two hours at a time now. Small victories, right?

Daniel's still working a lot, though. We've been distant, both of us lost in this new life we're building. But I know we'll get back to each other eventually.

Closing the book quickly, I decide that talking to Chase seems far more appealing. I grab my phone and dial his number. It rings for what feels like an eternity before he finally picks up, sounding slightly breathless.

"Avery. Hi," he says, his voice warm but hurried.

"Now a bad time?" I ask, a hint of teasing in my tone.

"No, I just ran out of the shower when I heard my phone ring," he replies.

"Waiting for someone specific? I feel like you could have just waited until after your shower?" I challenge playfully.

"Nah, I gave you a different ringtone on my phone, so I knew it was you." He says it so nonchalantly that I wonder if he knows my heart is bursting at the admission.

"How early aughts of you," I reply, trying to cover my sudden burst of warmth.

He chuckles. "Tell me about it."

"What are you doing? You ran off pretty quickly after dinner."

"Yeah," I drag out. "Long day."

"And now?" he asks back.

"Just wanted to talk." I sigh, hoping he doesn't ask anything further, not that I'd blame him, but he doesn't.

"Two truths and a lie?" he asks, and I smile.

"Yes."

At some point during the conversation, I must fall asleep. I wake up at 2 a.m. to the sound of Chase's gentle snoring coming through the phone's speaker. Squinting at the bright screen, I see the call time has stretched past five hours.

I smile and settle back into my pillow, letting my eyes drift closed once more.

CHAPTER ELEVEN

Avery

Three weeks later

The arena is swarming with kids and their parents. The hockey clinic is wrapping up, and it's gone perfectly. I arrived in the morning, making sure all the vendors had everything they needed. Then I ensured all parents got to their seats and were given their swag bags. The event adrenaline was pumping and I was excited all morning. Once the guys got on the ice with all the kids I could finally relax and watch.

Now that the clinic is over, it's time to let the players change and eat before they are back at the rink in two and a half hours for the charity game. As we predicted, having the game be between current and retired Devils players was a huge draw and we sold out the arena. That's $100 per ticket for all 20,000 seats.

I smile knowing we'll reach our goal for this event.

I finish helping one of our vendors when I see Chase standing in the corner, waiting for me, so I walk over to him. "Hey, how are you? The clinic was great."

Chase and I have only grown closer these past few weeks. We eat almost every meal together, and we've fallen asleep on the phone more than once. Last night, he showed up at my door with ice cream and his laptop, ready to stream *Transformers*. In addition to the ice cream, he also brought me a jersey stitched with his last name and number on the back. The charity game's theme is the jersey of your favorite NY Devils player. Since we will have so many current and past players, it's a great way to fill the arena with all the new and old jerseys.

I told him I have to stay professional through the whole event and that wearing a jersey isn't appropriate. He knew it was bullshit but he didn't push, and it made it harder. It feels like I'm disappointing him, but now, seeing him standing here, I'm more disappointed in myself for not bringing the jersey with me today.

"It was amazing. You killed it." His smile and tone are genuine.

"Well, this was the easy part for me. It was ninety percent planned by the time I came aboard. Everything from here is on my shoulders."

I feel his hand underneath my chin as he tilts my head up. "It's going to be amazing. *You* are amazing," he says, emphasizing the "you" in his statement.

"Thank you," I say.

He slowly pulls his hand away and I immediately missed his touch. I watch as his eyes graze over me. "Nice blazer."

I roll my eyes. "Thank you. You should go grab some food before you have to get back. Plus, I have work to do."

"All right, go kill it." He raises his hand in a fist, and I meet his with my own.

"I'll be cheering you on out there."

After he's out of sight, I pull my phone out of my back pocket and send a quick text to Jemmeye.

> **Me:** I need a favor.

> **Jemmeye:** Of course! What do you need?

> **Me:** Can you stop at my hotel before you come to the arena?

***

Jemmeye is at the arena within the hour, gripping the jersey Chase gave me last night. Her blonde curls bounce rhythmically with every confident step. She's sporting a jersey with Riley's signature sprawled across the chest, the fabric stretched snugly over her athletic frame.

You look terrific," I say, wrapping my arms around her in a quick hug.

"Avs, do you know what jersey this is?" Jemmeye asks, her eyes sparkling with enthusiasm as she completely ignores my compliment.

I look down at the jersey. "One of Chase's," I start, still a bit hazy. "He gave it to me last night."

She raises an eyebrow. "This is Chase's rookie year jersey!"

"Okayyy..." I drag the word out slowly, still not quite understanding what she's insinuating.

Jemmeye shakes her head dramatically, clearly on the verge of a lecture. "Okay, I know you don't know much about hockey, WAG traditions, or anything remotely related to sports. Honestly, it's kind of shocking that you're hosting anything related to sports right now," she says, stopping in her tracks for a moment, her arms crossed and rolling her eyes before trying to get back on track. "But the point is—this rookie jersey, it's—" She throws her hands up in the air as if searching for the right words. "It's sacred! It's like giving the cheerleader your varsity jacket in high school, or I don't know—giving someone a wedding ring!"

I snort, a little skeptical, and mutter, "Well, I feel like those are two pretty different extremes."

She shoots me a glare, her eyes narrowing. "My point is that Chase gave you his rookie jersey. He likes you. And I know you've got this little bet going on—on who will cave first—but he really likes you, Avery." Her tone softens, becoming almost tender. "Do you like him?"

"Of course I like him, Jemm. But my divorce is still a hot mess, and we're stuck working together for another six weeks. It's just messy, and I don't want to drag him into that..." I pause, then add quickly, "Plus, I don't like losing, so there's no way I'm not winning this bet."

Jemmeye bursts into laughter, her head tipping back as she lets out a genuine belly-deep laugh. "I knew I was going to love you," she says between giggles, her laughter contagious. After a few moments, she regains her composure. "But what if he sees this as you caving?"

I smirk, unbothered by the thought. "I'll tell him I call this good gameplay."

She nods approvingly. "All right, so what's the plan?"

***

I spend the whole game running around, making sure everything goes smoothly, and the little bit of the game I am able to catch, Chase scores. At the end of the third period, the "old dogs"—as the retired players like to refer to themselves—win 3–2. For a charity game, it's a nail-biter and has everyone on their seats.

Now, after the game, the players are signing jerseys and taking pictures before we wrap for the night, and technically my work obligations for the night are done. I take Chase's jersey in my hand as I slip into the bathroom closest to where all the players are, taking my blazer off and throwing the jersey over my camisole. I look at myself in the mirror and pull the collar up to my nose to smell it. It fills my nostrils with wood and cherry, and I have to fight the urge to wrap my arms around myself.

I nod in the mirror. "You got this. Good gameplay. It's all for fun and games." I walk out the door and get in the line where Jemmeye is waiting and holding our place.

When I join her, she smiles widely. "You look good." She nods. "Chase is going to die."

"I know." I smirk.

We finally make it to the front of the line, and Riley is the first to spot us. His gaze locks onto Jemmeye and brightens at the sight of her. And then, as if snapping out of his daydream, he notices me standing beside her. His eyes flick down to the jersey I'm wearing and then quickly back up to Jemmeye. A wide grin spreads across his face, and he can't hold it in—he bursts out laughing.

He quickly regains his composure, but not before Chase hears and glances up from where he's been chatting with another fan. His gaze finds mine almost immediately and time seems to stretch as his eyes lock with mine. My heart skips a beat, and then I watch his eyes slowly, deliberately, trail down my body. The jersey clings to my curves, the fabric taut over my chest. I see the recognition flash in his eyes, followed by something deeper—a look that sends a rush of heat through my veins. It's desire, raw and unfiltered. For a second, I think maybe I bit off more than I can chew. Is this good gameplay, or am I about to cave right here?

The moment feels surreal, the crowd buzz fading into the background as I lock eyes with him again. I smile, and trying to sound confident and sexy, despite the flutter in my stomach, I say, "Chase Matthews, you're easily my favorite player. Will you sign my jersey?"

His lips curve into a smile that makes my heart skip again, but then he leans forward slightly, placing a steady hand on my shoulder to balance himself as he bends over the table. The motion is fluid and effortless. I feel the warmth of his touch even through the fabric of my shirt, and I can't help but notice the faint rush of his breath against my skin as he reaches for the marker.

"Absolutely," he responds, his voice smooth and low, almost as if he's savoring the moment. I hear a slight hitch in his breath—he feels it too. His eyes flicker to mine as he carefully signs his name across the jersey fabric. Once he finishes, he lifts his head and leans in, his lips brushing my cheek in a swift, almost teasing kiss.

"And now it's yours, mystery girl," he murmurs, his voice a low, intimate whisper meant only for me. For a second, I forget about the bet, the game, and all I can focus on is the heat in his eyes and the way my nickname rolls off his tongue.

I move on quickly, letting the next person in line step forward, offering a hasty excuse to Jemmeye before I bolt for the door, eager to escape. I need to get away, to put distance between myself and Chase. I can feel the pull—the magnetic force between us— and I know that if I stayed any longer, I'd crumble. I'd give in. I'd give him anything he wanted.

Chase has been a complete enigma, something I can't quite figure out. Statistically speaking, he should be just another player—another hotshot athlete with an ego the size of the arena. He should be an asshole, the kind of guy who takes what he wants without a second thought.

But the thing is, I haven't found one single red flag about him. Not a single moment that makes me question his intentions, and that almost scares me more.

After a long hot shower, I slip into the familiar comfort of Chase's jersey, the fabric warm against my skin. I head over to my desk, trying to focus on the task at hand. We won't have the final numbers from the event until tomorrow at the earliest, but the urge to check my email is overwhelming. I open my inbox, scanning through the messages with a mix of anticipation and resignation, but it's all empty. No reports, nothing urgent.

I let out a sigh, my fingers hovering over the keyboard for a moment, but then my gaze shifts to the stack of my mother's journals sitting quietly on the corner of my desk. Do I want to ruin what's been a perfectly successful night by diving into the ghosts of my past?

But I can't stop myself. I pick up the book, fingers tracing the worn edges of the pages, and open to the last entry I left off on.

January 17th, 1993

I don't know how this happened. I'm only 10 weeks post-partum. I didn't think you could even get pregnant again this soon. We've only had sex once, and it was arguably the most uncomfortable sex of my life. My body doesn't feel anything like it used to, and now I'm pregnant again. What if my body can't take it?

Daniel is being great, saying that now we will have two kids so close in age that they will be best friends. I get it; I agree, but what about me? What if my body can't take it again?

February 14th, 1993

Daniel is taking me on a beautiful dinner date tonight, and my mom is coming in to babysit. I'm grateful, but I also feel awful. My body hurts, my boobs are sore, and now I need to squeeze into a dress and look pretty without the benefit of being able to eat the food I want or have a goddamn dirty martini.

March 1st, 1993

I must've done something in my past life, and I want to put down on paper that I apologize. Perhaps the winds can change, and I can stop being punished now.

I had my first doctor's appointment and am pregnant with twins.

The book drops from my hands, and I find it hard to breathe. If this is March of '93, this is when she was pregnant with Anthony. *We never knew Anthony was a twin.* My stomach turns, knowing where these journal entries are going to lead, and I hesitantly flip through a couple of pages of entries between the pregnancy and September '93, when Anthony was born.

September 10th, 1993

I don't know what to do, so I'm writing. But I don't know what to write. I feel numb, and when I don't feel numb, my heart feels broken. This should have been a beautiful week—the week we completed our family. A wife, a husband, and three beautiful children, and now we have a broken woman, a quiet man, a newborn without his sister he grew in the womb with, and an almost one-year-old who is relying on two people who are barely hanging on.

This wasn't supposed to be us. A surprise pregnancy—sure. A dead baby because of a botched doctor who wasn't prepared—no.

And now what? I can't be sad, upset, or mourn the daughter I never knew. I just have to get up and take care of my kids.

I sigh, closing the book and wiping my tears, tracing my cheeks as a new emotion I've never felt toward my mother swarms my thoughts: pity.

CHAPTER TWELVE

Chase

In the last six weeks, I've learned a few very important things about the mystery girl who lives in the Four Seasons, also known as the beautiful Avery Keenan.

One: She's fearless. I have not seen a single moment when she wasn't ready to tackle any situation head-on. Two: She's hilarious. I may even say funnier than me, but let's not get carried away. Three: She likes to play games, just like me.

First, she took our little bet so fast, and I saw the spark in her eye. She didn't just want to play, she wanted to win. And then the little stunt—showing up in my rookie jersey I gave her and having me sign her chest in front of all those people. I even tried to talk to Jemmeye, and all she said was, "It's good gameplay."

So *my girl* wants a game. She's got one.

I have a plan. I thought about it all night. Now, it's time to execute. Step one: get the guys on board. I pull out my phone and go to our bros only group chat—name courtesy of James after he sent a picture of the rash he had on his ass from his new pads in the group chat with Jemmeye and Avery.

> **Me:** I have 6 tickets to the UFC fights tonight downtown. Y'all in? Jemmeye too?

> **Riley:** Asking Jem!

> **James:** Hell yeah.

> **Billy:** What if I had a date and you only got six tickets?

> **Me:** I would sacrifice my ticket for your date so you would forgive me.

> **Billy:** Good answer. I, however, have no one.

> **James:** Yeah, no shit.

> **Riley:** We are in. Assuming the 6th is Avs?

> **Me:** Yep. She just doesn't know yet. The car will be ready at 7. See y'all then.

Step one: Complete.

Step two: Get Avery to say yes.

This is going to require more than just a text message. I quickly change and make my way to her room, unexpected nerves bubbling inside me as I knock on the door. When it swings open, I see her standing there—no makeup, just jeans and an old band t-shirt, and every-thing fades away around me. I'm such a goner for this girl, I can't even hide it.

A smile spreads across my face as my hand instinctive-ly reaches for her. She doesn't pull away as I rest my hand on her hip, leaning against the doorframe, savoring the warmth of her skin beneath mine.

"Hi." She giggles. "What are you doing here?"

"Oh yeah," I say, remembering the reason I came down here. "I got distracted—you're fucking gorgeous, did you know that? Anyway"—I shake my head—"do you have plans tonight? Do you want to come somewhere with me?"

"Caving already?" she teases with a playful smile.

"Oh, baby, if you would let me cave, I would be on my knees right now, but we already know this is all in your hands," I say matter-of-factly, and I see she's stunned by my honesty. But ever since I met Avery, we've always been straightforward with each other. I have no reason to hide how much I want her, and I'm more than willing to wait.

Of course, I plan to make it difficult, which is why I continue. "That being said, it's a group activity—the guys, you know, your best friends?" I say with a pointed look. "And Jemmeye."

She laughs. "Yeah, okay. I'm in. Where are we going?"

"We have floor tickets to the UFC fights tonight," I say, anticipating her reaction. "You said you like single-person sports, and I just so happen to have an in with a couple of fighters tonight."

Her face tightens just enough that I might have missed it if I weren't so mesmerized by every little movement she makes. "Who's the lead card?" she asks, forcing a smile that feels like it's meant to resemble her usual genuine one, but it looks nothing like it.

"Tony Kee and Dustin Belks. Do you not like UFC?" I ask quickly. "I can sell the tickets, and we can do something else tonight." I want to see this fight—the preliminary matches are supposed to be incredible too, but I'd cancel it all in an instant if Avery says she isn't interested.

"No," she says, taking a step forward and letting her genuine smile show. "I would love to go. What time should I be ready?"

Once again, a smile spreads across my face as I lean down to place a gentle kiss on her cheek. "I'll be back at your room at 6:45 p.m."

★★★

Here's the deal—I'm a solid six-foot-two and a pro athlete, so I'm not used to vying for the least desirable seat. But squeezing into a tight spot with Avery sounds perfect.

Riley texts me to say they're pulling up, and we head outside. Billy is in the front seat, while Riley, Jemmeye, and James occupy the second row. James hops out and slides the seat forward, revealing the third row.

"Last to be picked up, last to get good seats," he teases.

Avery glances at me, and I simply shrug. "It's the rules."

She rolls her eyes and slides into the back seat, with me following behind her. There's no way we can sit back here without our legs brushing against each other or our arms touching—exactly what I want. I notice her cheeks flush and I can't help but love it. I let my hand rest on her thigh, watching to see if she'll push it away, but she just leaves it there. My body is buzzing from the constant contact with Avery, and I know she feels it too. I watch as her chest starts to rise and fall rapidly as I paint designs across her skin with my finger.

The music blares, and everyone sings and dances to whatever Billy has on the playlist. Riley turns around, passing the flask back to us, and catches sight of my hand resting on Avery's thigh. He quickly turns away with a knowing smirk. Avery takes a large gulp from the flask before handing it to me. My hand never leaves her leg as we finish the flask between us.

When we finally arrive at the arena, everyone except Billy is thoroughly buzzed and bouncing with energy. This is why I love live sporting events—and probably why I chose to be part of the professional sports industry. The adrenaline of being in the same space as these high-intensity events makes my blood pump. The atmosphere is electric, filled with excitement and anticipation, and I can feel it coursing through me as we step out of the car and into the vibrant crowd.

My protectiveness kicks in as we walk through the entrance, and I keep my hand firmly entwined with Avery's. While I love UFC, and the energy of live events is unmatched, they also attract a more intimidating crowd.

My eyes stay locked in on Avery, wanting to make sure she feels safe and comfortable since I'm still not sure why she hesitated earlier when she found out we were coming here.

As the preliminary fights kick off, the atmosphere crackles with energy, and everyone is absolutely buzzing with excitement. Riley, Billy, Jemmeye, James, Avery, and I are all swept up in the hype, and the energy in the air is contagious.

James, always the life of the party, is leading the charge, fist-pumping and shouting at the screen, fully immersed in the action. His enthusiasm spreads quickly, and before long we are right there with him. Jemmeye is in her element, clapping and cheering after every punch thrown, even though it's clear she doesn't have a clue what's going on, but that doesn't stop her from getting caught up in the fun, laughing loudly and high-fiving the rest of us.

Even Billy, who's usually more subdued, has his eyes wide with excitement, grinning like a kid at a candy store. He nudges Riley playfully, and the two of them start bickering good-naturedly over who made the best fight predictions. Riley, ever the show-off, takes it as an opportunity to remind us all that his "undefeated streak" in fight predictions is legendary, flashing a smug smile as if it's some kind of championship title.

Jemmeye and Avery have been laughing non-stop, and I can't help but smile, relieved to see Avery enjoying herself. The crowd's roar intensifies as the fighters enter the ring for the main event, the anticipation building. But as soon as Tony Kee steps into the octagon I notice the shift. Avery's body tenses beside me, and the hand that's been securely wrapped in mine all night drops.

As the fighters take their positions, Avery's eyes remain glued to the octagon. Jemmeye must also notice the palpable shift in the air. She glances at me, her expression questioning as if to ask what's happened. I shrug and redirect my focus to Avery.

I gently sway, bumping my hip against hers, hoping to pull her back into the moment. But she doesn't budge, lost in whatever thoughts are swirling in her mind. I can feel the tension radiating off her, making my stomach tense. The crowd roars as the bell rings, and I do my best to pull my attention off of her and onto the fight.

Tony and Dustin begin walking toward each other, bouncing on the balls of their feet, daring one another to make the first move. I catch a glimpse of Tony scanning the crowd, and to my surprise, his gaze lands on Avery. It feels like time stops—Avery and Tony are locked in, and he's distracted, giving Dustin the immediate advantage.

Tony shakes his head, regaining focus. The fight is intense, but my attention is divided. I steal glances at Avery, who's gone stiff and closed off. It's clear that the sight of Tony has unsettled her, and it's clearly done the same to Tony, who is fighting like a rookie. As the round ends, I watch him sink onto the stool, getting patched up. Neither of us takes our eyes off him.

Then I see it—Tony leans in, whispering something to his trainer, who suddenly looks our way. I feel a knot tighten in my stomach. Almost immediately, the trainer approaches us, and I prepare myself for whatever's coming next.

"He wants to talk to you," he says, directing his attention toward Avery.

"What? No," I respond instinctively, reaching out for her. But she pulls her arm close, indicating she's not interested. I feel our friends' eyes on us, but I can't bring myself to look. I'm so thrown off and slightly embarrassed to realize I'm just as in the dark as they are.

Avery sighs, her expression unreadable, and then without another word, she walks away, leaving the rest of us—especially me—dumbfounded. I watch her go, my mind racing with questions and an overwhelming urge to stop her, but all I can do is stand here.

Chapter Thirteen

Avery

My legs feel heavy as I go over to where my brother is getting stitched up. I didn't know how he'd react upon seeing me—if he'd even see me. I intended to lie low and watch from a distance, but front-row seats made that nearly impossible.

Anthony's expression is unreadable, but given how shaken he was from seeing me, nearly getting knocked out—I can't imagine he's happy. Suddenly, I feel like a little kid again, desperately seeking my brother's attention and affection.

"Heyyy," I draw out, trying to lighten the mood.

He leans against the corner of the octagon, a mix of annoyance and surprise on his face. "What the hell, Avs? Couldn't give me a heads-up you'd be here?"

"I'm sorry! I didn't find out until a few hours ago," I say defensively. "And it's not like we text," I add, a hint of sarcasm creeping in.

He glances back toward Chase and my friends, his brow furrowing. "Who's the linebacker who looks like he wants to kill me?"

A small smile breaks across my face. "Hockey player, actually. That's Chase. He's a friend."

"Where's Campbell?"

"Filed for divorce," I reply plainly, earning me another shocked reaction from Anthony. "Listen, I could fill you in on the shitshow that is my life, but I think you're in the middle of something." I nod toward Dustin Belks, who looks like he's running out of patience.

"Will you stay and watch from here? I've never had anyone besides Gary stand in my corner," he mutters, glancing toward his trainer. I see the vulnerability in his eyes, and it hits me hard.

We're the same—honestly, all four of us probably are—desperately craving support and love but not knowing how to ask for it or even show it ourselves. My heart cracks at the thought of him feeling as alone as I've felt before and him not having anyone.

"Of course I will," I say, placing my hand on his sweaty forearm. "Now, please go win and impress your little sister and her friends."

He smirks and turns toward Dustin, ready for round two.

I try to keep my focus on my brother and the fight unfolding before me, but I can't help glancing over at Chase, who hasn't taken his eyes off me since I walked away. I know he's confused. I didn't mention I know who Tony Kee is when he told me about the lead card, and I doubt he's connected the dots that Tony Kee is short for Anthony Keenan.

While entirely unnecessary, the jealousy etched across his face brings a small thrill. It's nice to know he cares, even if it's in a misguided way. It makes me feel wanted and desired. I intend to clear up the confusion as soon as I walk over to him, but for now I'm secretly enjoying the moment.

As the fight progresses, the intensity in the arena reaches a fever pitch. Tony and Dustin exchange fierce blows, each punctuated by the crowd's roar. Unlike round one, Anthony is at the top of the game, a smug smile tattooed on his face. I feel his energy pulsating through me as he dances around the ring, slipping past Dustin's defenses with agility and precision. The moment he lands a solid right hook, I can't help but cheer, my heart racing with each punch.

The time between the second and third rounds is quick. I keep a hand on his shoulder as Gary rubs Vaseline on a cut that has now formed above his eyebrow. As the round begins, I watch Anthony channel everything he has left into a stunning combination that leaves Dustin staggering and then passing out cold on the floor. When the referee finally raises Tony's hand in victory, the arena erupts in a deafening cheer, and I can't help but feel a rush of pride for my brother.

As he stands there, catching his breath, I glance back at Chase and realize that the whole group is watching me. I laugh, waving my hand to invite them over. Chase wastes no time beelining it toward me, with everyone else falling shortly behind him as they try to weave through the crowd.

Chase makes it to me as soon as Anthony returns to the corner.

"Chase." I smile. "Meet Anthony, my older brother. Anthony, meet my...friend, Chase."

"Your brother," Chase says, smiling, as I watch the tension melt from his body at the realization.

"My brother," I confirm, just as the rest of the group arrives.

"Your brother?" Billy questions. "See, Chase, you can stop crying now. He's not competition who could kill you with his bare hands. It's just her protective older brother who could kill you with his bare hands. That's much better!"

"Nice fight, man," James says to Anthony.

"Thanks, man." He nods before turning his attention to me. "I, uh, gotta go. I have some other shit I have to handle tonight, but thanks for coming."

Again, that vulnerability is heartbreaking. "I'm going to start coming to a lot more."

He smiles. "All right, I gotta go." He puts a hand in my hair and ruffles it, making me playfully shove him off.

I watch as he takes a few steps, and our mother's journals flash in my mind.

"Anthony!" I shout, taking a few quick steps toward him. He turns around quickly at the sound of my voice.

"What's up?"

"Can we grab lunch next week? I want to catch up and tell you about some stuff," I say.

"Uh, yeah. For sure. Just text me when and where, and I'll make it work," he says.

"Okay, I'll text you tomorrow. Good fight, big brother."

He smiles and turns back around, walking away.

***

After the fight, the six of us find a local bar and burst through the door like bulls in a china shop. It's the kind of dive that smells like beer and old wood, with faded sports memorabilia on the walls, and a lone bartender who looks both thrilled and terrified to see us.

Chase and Billy immediately head to the bar, pulling out their wallets to pay the tabs of the six solitary drinkers scattered around the place. Their generosity earns us smiles and even a thumbs-up from one of the regulars nursing a whiskey in the corner.

It doesn't take long for us to charm the owner into dusting off the old karaoke machine in the corner, which leads us to this moment of Riley and Jemmeye absolutely butchering "Angel" by Sarah McLachlan while ripping back tequila shots.

I'm at a back table with Chase, clutching my stomach as I laugh so hard I'm almost positive I will pee my pants. Meanwhile, Billy and Jamie are deep in a poker game with an older guy in the corner, who looks like he's been playing cards since the Nixon administration.

After a solid five minutes, I'm able to pull myself together and my laughter starts to fade. When I glance over at Chase, he's looking at me. His face is flushed from the shots we've been taking, and his eyes are sparkling under the dim bar lights. His smile is wide, and I feel my core start to throb at the sight. I have to physically hold my hand down to not touch him.

"Thank you for tonight," I say softly, my voice breathless. "I needed this."

"Anytime, sweetheart," he replies, his voice low and sincere.

My grin grows. "Want to take more shots?" I ask.

I'm having fun and I don't want to stop. Typically, drinking always ends up with fights with Campbell or crying. But right now, with Chase and his friends, I'm just having fun.

Chase laughs, shaking his head. "On a scale of one to ten, how drunk are you?"

"Hmm." I tilt my head, pretending to consider the question. "A solid six. But don't worry, I'm a grown woman and can cut myself off, thank you very much."

He laughs again. "All right, your wish is my command. I'll be right back."

He stands to head to the bar, but before he can take a step, I jump up, dramatically whining, "No, no, I'm coming with you."

I stumble slightly and my hand automatically reaches for his. The moment my fingers wrap around his, warmth floods my chest, and my thighs are aching. I need another shot or I'm about to give in to this bet way too quickly.

"You're adorable, baby," he murmurs as he pulls me into him.

"I know," I joke with a shrug and head toward the bar, tugging Chase behind me.

***

An hour and five shots later, we're piled into the car, our driver taking us all back home. Chase and I are tucked into the back seat, while Jemmeye and Riley occupy the row in front of us, still belting out karaoke songs at full volume. Jamie and Billy are sprawled in the bucket seats ahead of them, laughing over something I can't quite hear.

I'm leaning into the corner of the seat, my legs draped over Chase's lap, his warm hand trailing lazy circles up and down my thigh. I thought the more shots I took, the drunker I'd feel, but I'm still hovering at a solid six—except on the horny scale, where I'm skyrocketing to at least a twelve.

The car is dimly lit, shadows flickering from the passing streetlights, and the chaos of the singing and laughter drowns out any sound I might make. My body buzzing with liquid courage, I lean forward and rest my head against Chase's chest, tilting my face to meet his gaze with wide, innocent eyes.

"Hi," I whisper, my voice light and breathless.

"Hi, baby," he murmurs, a mischievous smile playing at his lips. "Whatcha doing?"

My hand falls to his pants and my fingers toy with the zipper. "Just to be clear," I start looking up at him again, "this is not me caving or giving in to the bet."

"What's not?" he asks, and even though I can't see him in the darkness of the car, I can hear in his raspy response and growing cock that he's turned on just as much as I am.

I slide the zipper down slowly, the sound loud in the quiet bubble of our corner of the car. My fingers move deliberately to the button at his waist, unfastening it with a small, satisfying pop. Chase lifts his hips just slightly, a silent invitation, as I tug his pants down a fraction, the fabric bunching at his hips.

My hands slip under the waistband of his boxers, the warmth of his skin making my own fingertips tingle. He jolts slightly at the touch, his muscles tightening under my hands.

"Sorry, my hands are cold," I murmur into his ear, my lips brushing against the shell as I speak.

"Don't you dare apologize," he says.

My thighs ache, and I so badly want to get on top of him and straddle him, but I think that would definitely be caving. So instead, I take a page out of his playbook. My thumb rubs over the tip of his cock, spreading pre-cum over the head. I dip my head and slowly take his dick in my mouth.

He moans, and I immediately shoot up, covering his mouth with my hand.

"If you want this, you have to be quiet. Nod if you understand," I whisper, earning me a nod back.

I slowly remove my hand, and he pulls my head to his lips. "What's gotten into you tonight, mystery girl? How did I get so lucky?" He sounds like he's in disbelief.

"Just roll with it." I laugh softly, trying to play it cool even as my heart pounds. I lean forward, just about to let myself get lost in Chase again, when the singing abruptly stops.

Riley spins around in his seat, his head whipping back to look at us. Panic shoots through me like a bolt of lightning, and I instinctively throw myself into a casual sprawl, legs still draped over Chase's bare thighs—and, conveniently, directly over his very obvious boner.

"What song would you both like next?" Riley asks, clearly oblivious to the situation.

I clamp my lips shut, biting back the breathlessness in my voice.

Chase doesn't miss a beat. "Literally anything. Just keep it going," he says, his voice steady and deceptively calm.

Satisfied, Riley turns back around, and moments later the opening notes of "Let It Go" from *Frozen* blares through the speakers.

Chase's hand shoots out, grabbing my arm and pulling me upright. I think he's about to kiss me, but instead, he leans in close, his breath hot against my ear. "Just to be clear," he murmurs, his tone dripping with mischief. "If Riley hadn't cock-blocked me just now, that would've counted as caving, beautiful."

I huff, leaning back. Adrenaline is still pumping from almost getting caught. It was terrifying, but I kind of liked it. I never tried anything sexually with Campbell. We were about as vanilla as it got, and with Chase I feel like I'm on drugs, desperate to get a fix.

But Chase is technically right. A blow job would easily be considered caving. But with the alcohol still running through me, the adrenaline of everyone being in the car, and Chase's throbbing dick I feel on the back of my legs, I can't help myself.

"You're right," I say, causing Chase to look over at me, and all of a sudden my skirt is a great idea. My hands lift up my skirt and I slide Chase's hand up my thigh right before he can touch my core and then I slide my hand down my soaked slits. His hand I'm holding in place grips my flesh to almost a painful degree, but it only makes me move faster. My fingers move around my clit and after a moment I have to take my hand off Chase's to cover my mouth from the noises I can't stop. He puts his other hand on my other thigh, so close my knuckles graze his, and I know he can feel the heat coming from me.

I'm so close, I take Chase's hand and put it over mine, and the mere pressure sends me over the edge. Chase grabs my hand almost immediately, licking it clean, and I swear it's the hottest thing I've ever seen. My adrenaline is fading and the liquid courage I've been riding is rapidly wearing off.

Luckily, within minutes, the car pulls up to the hotel. After a chaotic scramble of climbing over seats, exchanging sloppy, drunken hugs, and waving off Jemmeye's endless chatter about the next karaoke night, Chase and I finally make it into the elevator.

I lean against the wall, my eyes fluttering closed—not just because I'm desperate for sleep but because I know Chase is standing there with a smug grin plastered across his face. The soft ding of the elevator pulls me back and I peek one eye open. We've reached my floor.

With a sigh, I force myself to look at him. As expected, he's wearing a shit-eating grin.

I roll my eyes, stepping off the elevator. "Like I said, that was *not* caving to the bet."

"Mm-hmm," he hums, leaning casually against the doorframe as the elevator doors start to close. "Good night, mystery girl."

I pause, letting his voice linger for a second before turning away. "Good night, Chase."

Walking down the hall, I can still feel his gaze on me, that stupid grin burning into the back of my mind.

CHAPTER FOURTEEN

Avery

It's been one week since seeing my brother and having a drunk, sloppy hookup with Chase in the back of a rented car. *Wow, if I had said that sentence to myself even a couple of months ago, I would've thought I was going insane.*

I've spent the last seven days feverishly reading through my mother's journals from when Anthony was born. It's been awful and life-changing. She lost a child and had to move forward, raising another while having an almost-toddler. It sounds terrifying, and if I know anything about my father, he probably didn't help. There's no doubt she was suffering from postpartum depression along with grieving such a loss, but back in the '90s, no one was talking about postpartum. And from the sound of it, mothers had it even harder than they do now. It doesn't erase my mother being shitty most of her life, but I guess it makes me understand her more.

I deserved more, but maybe so did she.

I wipe my palms down my jeans as I walk into the diner. I've never just met my brother for lunch before, let alone eaten with him anywhere under a Michelin-starred restaurant. The only time we ever went out to eat as a family was for holidays.

There's a heaviness on my chest that feels like a strange mixture of excitement and anxiety.

My eyes scan the red leather booths. I sort of hope I'm here first to give myself more time to gain my composure, but I also don't want to go through the anxiety of thinking my brother might stand me up. After my eyes filter through almost the whole restaurant, my eyes land on him. He's at a small booth near the back, a ball cap riding low on his head and wearing a fitted black hoodie. His gaze stays fixated on his phone, and I fight the urge to turn and run out of the building.

Come on, Avery. You can do this. He's your brother, for God's sake.

My legs wobble slightly as I make my way over to him. "Hey," I say, placing a hand softly on his shoulder.

He looks up and gives me a small smile. I slide into the booth seat across from him. I don't know where to start—I find my brain going through all the scenarios in my head, and none end with anything but Anthony getting up and storming out of here. As I rattle through my brain for some mind-blowing answer, Anthony's voice pulls me out of my internal battle.

"Avs? You good?" His voice is laced with concern, and I find myself squinting, studying his face.

"Yeah, I'm nervous," I admit.

"Me too." He nods.

Before we can say anymore, a spunky blonde waitress is at our table with a coffee pot and a notepad. "Good morning, y'all! Coffee?"

We nod silently, and she pours our coffee before handing us two menus. "Is there anything else I can get you at the moment?" she asks, not losing a smidge of her enthusiasm.

"No, all set," I reply, but she doesn't move. Instead, she stares at Anthony, ogling at him as he stares down, oblivious that the girl just wants his attention. I roll my eyes and kick his shin under the table.

"Hey, what the fuck?" he yelps in shock, staring at me wide-eyed.

I give him a smirk and give a quick nod to the waitress.

"Oh, uh, yeah, sorry, sweetheart, I need a couple of minutes as well."

The waitress smiles at him, using a nickname on her and bounces away, and for the second time in just as many minutes, I roll my eyes.

"Wow, one diner excursion with your brother and you learn so much," I mock, causing him to be now the one rolling his eyes. He takes a long sip of his coffee before looking back at me.

"So what's up, Avs? I know you didn't just invite me to breakfast to make awkward small talk," he says, keeping a hand on his coffee cup, letting his finger slowly tap the side.

"Would it be so weird if I did want to just go to breakfast with my brother?" I challenge.

"You never have before."

"Neither have you."

We both stay silent until I finally can't stand the silence anymore. "Well, you're right. I did call you for a reason, but you're also wrong, Anthony. I know we've never been close. We weren't raised to be, and we can't change the past, but I want to be in your life. I want to be your sister in whatever fucked up sense that means for our family. Both of our parents are dead, you're single, I'm divorced. Abigail and Adam are alone, working thousand-hour weeks. I don't want us to be like them. I want to be your family." My voice cracks at the end and I feel the tears threatening to fill my eyes.

I wasn't planning to unload on him like that, but as soon as I started, I couldn't stop myself. Now he's staring at me like I have six heads, and I have to admit, I'm sort of regretting it.

"Anthony," I say slowly. "You gotta say something."

"You're my little sister, and I love you. I have no idea what that means or how to show it to you, but I do love you. So, yeah, let's be in each other's lives and try to be better than our parents," he says, nodding like he's trying to convince himself as much as he's trying to agree with me.

"Good, I'm glad we agree," I say before taking a deep breath and preparing myself. "Because now I need to tell you why I invited you here." I pause again, taking in Anthony's face. *Maybe I should back out. No, hell, you already love-bombed him, so why not throw some trauma on top?*

"So, after Mom's funeral, I went to their house alone and I found this box with a bunch of journals she wrote. I've only gone through a couple of them so far, but they seem to be from the years all of us were born, and well, they are insightful."

"What do you mean?" he asks.

"I don't know, the journals, Mom's writing. There were times when I was reading her writing from before Abigail, and even after Abigail was born...she seemed so happy, and she had these dreams and ideas," I say, shrugging my shoulders, not knowing how to continue.

"So, what changed? What turned the beautiful princess into the Wicked Witch of the West?" he asks with a laugh, but it's less humorous and more murderous. And again, I question if I should continue.

"Like I said, I haven't gotten past the second journal. I'm sure there's a lot that takes you from a happy twenty-year-old to a miserable, heartless middle-aged woman," I say, trying to make sure he knows I agree. She was awful and what I am about to say doesn't excuse how she neglected us emotionally. "But she had Abby so young, and you know dad wasn't helping, and then not even four months later she got pregnant again with you." I pause again. "Did she ever talk to you about when she was pregnant with you?"

He winces. "Eww. No, why?"

"Based on the journals, you were a twin." I say it slowly, trying to read his face for any acknowledgment that he knows this information.

"What?"

"You were a twin, but the baby died at birth. A weird, fucked up tragedy, I guess. Mom was a baby herself, was raising two kids, and grieving another. She doesn't say it, but the postpartum depression spills off the pages, she lost herself—and it's no excuse, but there was a reason." My voice is convincing and low as I continue. "She had this business plan of opening a bookstore that turned into a speakeasy in the evenings. Dad agreed, but then she got pregnant and he told her she had to stay home and raise the kids. She had no choice, she lost everything she was and took it out on us."

"So, moral of the story, Mom sucks but Dad sucks worse. Got it. Cool. Oh, and I had a twin, but they died." He bobs his head back and forth.

"That's what I know." I nod in agreement. I want to say more, but this is the most vulnerable I've been…ever…and my nerves are shot. "So, here's the thing…number one, I have the two journals. I think you should take them and read them, see her story in her own writing. Two, I have a proposition for you."

"Avs, I know we just got close and all, but I think you should typically ask for a favor before you trauma dump on their life."

I roll my eyes. "No favors, a proposition," I reiterate.

He lifts his hand and waves it, signaling for me to continue. "Mom talks about the exact building she wanted to buy for the speakeasy. I looked it up for shits and giggles, and it's for sale. I want to buy it and I want to make Mom's business a reality."

He stares at me dumbfounded. "This is some weird guilt, death grieving shit, isn't it? What do you know about opening a bookstore or a speakeasy?"

"Nothing." I shrug, leaning back in my chair. "And neither do you, but I think we can do it together."

"*Together?*" he shouts. "Why me?"

"Well, here's the deal...I actually want it to be the four of us all together, but I need you first so we can go buy the building and handle that aspect quickly before it's purchased by someone else. Then I need you to help convince Abby and Adam to join us."

He laughs before leaning back and looking around, presumably for our waitress, who I'm now realizing hasn't been back in a while. "And why would I do that? A woman who couldn't show her kids an ounce of love their whole lives, why would I do this?" His voice is high and angry, like a hurt kid.

"Maybe this is what she leaves us. A thirty-year-old business plan and four kids who desperately need a way to get closer. Pulling the journals from my bag, I wave them in the air. "This is it. The last thing from our shitty parents, but like I said, I want you in my life, and I think this is a way the four of us move forward."

He groans before burying his face in his hands. I let him decompress while I looked around, finally catching the eye of our waitress. She sees me and begins to bounce over.

"Hi, again! I wanted to make sure I gave you enough, and you guys seemed chatty! Are you ready now?" she asks.

"Yes, can I have the cheeseburger, a side of fries, and a chocolate milkshake?" I answer while handing my menu to Anthony.

He takes my menu, sets it on his own, and then looks up at his doe-eyed admirer. "I'll do the same. Thank you, sweetheart."

She blushes as she takes the menus from his hands, and I watch his fingers accidentally graze hers. They both linger a second too long, and I can't handle the tension. I quickly cough, and she jumps like I scared her and scurries off.

"Seriously, do you know this girl? What am I witnessing?" I ask in disbelief.

"I don't, but I might have to start," he says, watching her walk away, which causes me to kick my brother in the shin for the second time tonight.

Maybe we are getting used to this sibling thing quicker than I thought.

He shakes his head and refocuses on me. "You really want to do this?"

"Yes. I really do."

"Okay, let's do it."

CHAPTER FIFTEEN

Avery

I feel revitalized. Ever since lunch with Anthony, everything has felt lighter, as if things are about to change for the better. I catch my reflection in the mirror, a smile spreading across my face as I bask in the newfound brightness and confidence that seem to flow through me.

Today is packed with productive plans. First, I'm heading to the arena to ensure everything's in place for the charity tailgate next week. After that, I'll meet the realtor at the building to discuss the conditions.

And after I play boss lady all day, I'm planning to "accidentally" bump into Chase at the hotel bar for a dinner date. It's getting harder and harder to resist this man. I find myself trying to talk myself out of all the reasons I've been telling him and myself about why we can't do this.

Sure, Campbell and I are still technically married, but that's only because the little prick won't sign the papers.

He's gone out of his way to cancel my phone service, my health insurance, and even my Pilates membership, which I should've expected after he tried to cancel my credit cards. But I keep thinking—he's inconvenienced me enough for one lifetime. He has to be getting bored with it by now, right?

And yes, Chase and I still have about four weeks of working together, and the last thing I want is for anyone to think I'm unprofessional or risk losing the opportunity to run these charity events next year. But then he does something like push my hair out of my face while I'm rambling at the bar or leave little sticky notes with sweet one-liners on my door every morning—and I'm ready to say "screw it" and risk it all.

I mean, what is that?

I shake my head, trying to push thoughts of Chase to the back of my mind. That's something for later. Right now, it's all about work. I take a deep breath and swing my door open, only to stop dead in my tracks. There, across the hall, stands Chase. He's leaning casually against the wall, a small blue sticky note in hand with the words *spend the day with me* scrawled across it in his neat handwriting.

My breath catches in my throat, and for a moment it's like the world stops spinning. He's dressed in dark gray pants that fit him perfectly and a black t-shirt that clings just enough to highlight the defined muscles of his chest and the sharp curve of his biceps.

I can feel my heart race, my pulse quickening as my eyes involuntarily trace the lines of his body. My mouth goes dry, and I nearly have to pick it up off the floor as I stand frozen, caught between a smile and the overwhelming urge to step closer.

I quickly pull myself together, scraping my tongue across the roof of my mouth, desperate to keep my voice steady and not give away how ridiculously attractive I find him. He's easily the hottest man I've ever seen, and I'm doing everything to play it cool. With a cocky smirk, I tilt my head to the side and cross my arms. "You think you can just show up in a tight t-shirt and jeans that accentuate your ass, and I'll throw all my plans out the window? Mighty cocky, Chase." My voice drips with sarcasm, though I can't completely hide the flutter in my chest.

Chase throws his head back with a laugh that's deep and effortless, and once again I find myself mesmerized by how his chest rises and falls with each chuckle. For a brief moment, all I can think is how badly I wish his t-shirt would disappear. He takes a few quick steps forward, closing the distance between us until he's right in front of me. Without warning, he presses a soft kiss to my cheek, the warm sensation lingering after he pulls away. He places the sticky note into my hand, and I glance down at it, smiling before tucking it into the purse hanging over my shoulder.

"Never, sweetheart. I just want to tag along while you do your plans. If that's okay, of course."

I blink, caught off guard by the simplicity of his request. "Really? What if I planned to skip into the forest, talking to squirrels all day? You'd just want to tag along?"

His grin widens, and he shrugs, his tone playful yet sincere. "Yeah, that sounds great, actually. Are you really going to do that? If so, we should invite James—sounds like something right up his alley."

I can't help but laugh at the image of it. "Well, good to know. But unfortunately, it's not that exciting. I've got a few work errands to run."

His eyes light up, and he leans in slightly, his voice warm. "Do you want company?"

The question catches me off guard again, but I am smiling softly this time. Without thinking, I reach for his hand, my fingers brushing against his as I pull him toward the elevator. "Let's go."

***

Once we arrive at the arena, Chase gives me the space to handle everything. He heads to the locker room to check in with the team, leaving me to run through my list of tasks. I'm focused as I confirm with vendors, triple-check decorations, and ensure everything is set for the upcoming charity tailgate. An hour later, I finally head toward the locker rooms to find Chase and drag him to my next errand.

I know I will have to explain the details of the building we're going to see and why it's important, but the thought of it has my stomach tied in knots. The last thing I want is for him to know too much about my chaotic family situation. Chase has seen my messy side already—there's no hiding it after Campbell made a scene at the hotel bar. But I've gone out of my way to keep him from getting too involved in the mess that is my family.

From the way he talks about his own family, it's clear that the way we grew up couldn't be more different. He might as well be the poster child for Family Man of the Year. And me? I'm the spoiled rich girl from a broken home, surrounded by drama and dysfunction.

As much as I'm trying to keep Chase at arm's length, I can't help but worry—what will happen when he starts to learn more about my reality? Will he start to pull away? Because the more time we spend together, the harder it is to keep my walls up.

When I finally find Chase, he's in the video room, absorbed in footage from what looks like games from the previous season. I stand in the doorway momentarily, watching him as he stays laser-focused on the screen. His brows furrow in concentration, and I can't help but admire the way he locks into whatever he's doing. After a few seconds, I quietly take a few steps forward and lower myself onto the seat next to him.

"Hey." I smile softly, not wanting to startle him.

"Hey," he says, pausing the footage as his eyes flick toward me. "You finish up?"

"Yep, all done here," I reply, feeling the weight of everything I still need to say.

"So, what's next?" he asks, his voice casual with a hint of curiosity there.

I give a small smile, but it doesn't reach my eyes. I let out a breath, trying to steady myself. "Yeah... So, we're heading to a building that's for sale, closer to the East Side."

"Oh, yeah?" he says, his interest piqued. "Is it for you?"

"Well…" I stand up and start walking toward the door. Talking feels easier when I don't have to look him in the eye. "Yes, but not just me. Anthony, and maybe some of my other siblings, but they don't know yet."

He follows me, confusion flickering across his face. "Wait!" He catches up quickly, his voice more alert. "You have more siblings besides Anthony?"

"There are four of us total," I begin, my voice steady but carrying a weight I didn't expect. "Abigail—she's a partner at a law firm in the city. Anthony, whom you know now. Then there's Adam—he's a neurosurgery resident at Trinity Hospital on the East Side." I pause momentarily, glancing at him as I gesture toward myself. "And then me," I say, waving my hands down my body with a light laugh as if that sums it all up.

Chase takes a few quick steps forward, beating me to the main doors leading back to my car. He opens the door, leaning against the frame to let me pass through. "Is the building for you to live in?" he asks, his tone casual.

"Commercial, actually," I reply.

He hums in acknowledgment as if absorbing the information but not wanting to interrupt. I stay silent as we make our way to my car. Once we reach it, he opens the driver's side door, and I slide in, placing my hands on the steering wheel to steady myself. I take a deep breath, knowing I'm about to spill the whole truth.

"Here's the deal," I begin, my voice surprisingly steady. "My brother and I are trying to buy the building and start this library by day, speakeasy by night kind of business. It was my mom's dream, but she couldn't do it because she had four kids in four years, and my dad was kind of a dick. Now they're both dead, and we were never close, so...it's probably a grief-trauma response. But we're going to open the business for her."

I finally stop talking, my chest tight from the rush of words. I expect to look up at him and see a look of horror, maybe even pity—but when I do, I find his eyes bright, his smile wide.

"I like it," he says with a shrug. "A library with maybe a wine bar, and then a total bourbon club vibe at night? It's a great idea."

With that, he shuts the door and starts walking around to his side of the car.

I let out a breath, almost a laugh, and mutter, "He likes it." It feels like a weight has lifted, even if just a little, and I'm surprised by how much that matters to me.

Whenever I would talk to Campbell about event ideas or give him my thoughts on a new building he was buying, he would just brush me off or make it seem like my ideas were unrealistic. After a while, I stopped caring about his response, and soon after that, I stopped telling him my ideas altogether.

As Chase slides into the passenger seat, I feel a new sense of calm settle in, and I shift the car to drive. One night, when Chase and I were playing two truths and a lie, I confessed to him that I loved driving, that Campbell and even my family always had drivers, and while that does have a particular luxury, driving makes me feel in control. Maybe that's what gives me the confidence to keep spilling my guts to Chase on the drive to the building. The rhythmic hum of the car and the familiar sense of control make it easier to open up to him. With my hands on the wheel, I feel steady, like I can say whatever's been swirling around in my head without the fear of it all crashing down. So I keep talking, words tumbling out as effortlessly as the miles ticking by.

"Once we secure the building, Anthony and I are going to tell Abigail and Adam, and we think between the two of us we can convince them to join us in getting it started," I confess, keeping my eyes fixed on the road. The hum of the tires offers some comfort as I speak.

"What will you do if they say no?"

I glance at him. "I know it sounds..." I pause, searching for the right word. "Stupid, weird, I don't know, take your pick. But when my mom died, I didn't expect much to change. We were never close, and in the years before her passing, we spoke maybe a handful of times. But then I went to her funeral, and my world just...shattered. I left Campbell. I found these journals of hers. I met you..." I trail off, my throat tightening for a second. Glancing at him again, I add softly, "This feels like the last part. Connecting with my siblings, starting this business—this company that was my mom's dream. It feels like something I have to do."

"Then you're going to do it, Avs. You will figure out how to reconnect with the three of them, and you are going to open this killer place, and I will be your first customer. Plus, you know I will help you however you let me."

I laugh softly, the tension in my body easing with his words. "Okay, okay. Now, it's your turn. Tell me something about you so I don't feel embarrassed and exposed."

He doesn't hesitate, his voice calm but serious. "You never have to be embarrassed opening up to me, Avery."

I nod, my gaze focused on the road. "I know."

The silence stretches between us, comfortable but quiet, until I'm about to turn on the radio, desperate to fill the space. But then Chase speaks again, his voice soft, almost like he's testing the words before letting them slip out.

"I thought about quitting hockey when my dad died," he says, his voice thickening slightly. He pauses, and I hear the audible swallow that follows. "My family and I are so close. I thought when my dad died, they'd need me. My brother's married but still lives in the town we grew up in. When I went home for the funeral, I had every intention of quitting, but they convinced me not to give up on my dream. They were right, you know? Not to let me quit. But after the funeral, I only had a couple of days with them before I had to go back, and they all grieved together while I had to grieve alone. I don't know...it felt like they didn't need me. And I think that hurt, on top of everything else."

My heart clenches at his words. Without thinking, I take my hand off the steering wheel and gently place it in his, offering a soft squeeze. He doesn't pull away, and we sit like that, the quiet of the car wrapping around us.

When we pull up to the building, a short, stocky man is standing out front, his face inches from his phone as he stares intently at the screen. As soon as I shift the car into park, Chase is out the door and around to mine, opening it before I even have a chance to grab my purse.

We walk toward the man, and the moment he looks up from his phone his eyes widen in recognition.

"Chase Matthews from the New York Devils?" He practically beams with excitement, a huge grin forming across his face. "You're the one interested in this building?"

The energy in his voice is palpable as he extends his hand to Chase, who takes it with a firm shake.

"I'm just tagging along today," Chase says, his tone casual. "My gir—*friend*, Avery, is the one who coordinated this meeting."

Simon's attention shifts to me now, his eyes gleaming with curiosity. He steps forward, hand extended. "Simon Simmens. Nice to meet you, Avery."

"Nice to meet you as well," I reply with a smile, trying to keep my nerves under control. "I'm very interested in seeing the building and making an offer."

Simon's eyes light up at my directness, and he laughs. "A lady on a mission, okay! Let's go."

He fumbles for the keys in his pocket and when he finally unlocks it, I take a cautious step forward. The building is made of brick, worn and tired-looking. It feels like it's been waiting for something to bring it back to life. From my research, it's been vacant since COVID—before that, it housed a coffee shop, diner, and even a video store. Nothing has lasted longer than five years, but I can see *her* vision—the back wall lined with bookshelves, the bar that could wrap around the other side, dark leather seating.

As Simon leads us further, I clear my throat and speak up. "It's been on the market for three hundred thousand for the last eight months with no bites. Why aren't they dropping the price?"

Simon shrugs, his face unreadable. "The owners aren't desperate to sell. They'll part with it if the right offer comes, but they don't want to lose money."

"Mmm," I hum in acknowledgment, nodding thoughtfully. "I can offer three hundred twenty-five thousand if they're willing to close by the end of the month. I'll even waive inspections."

My voice is steady and confident, even though my heart is pounding. I'm praying I'm not giving away just how badly I need this place.

Simon's eyes flicker with surprise at my offer and he doesn't say anything for a moment. His hand is still resting on the doorframe as he considers my words, a small crease appearing between his brows.

"Waiving inspections, huh?" he asks, clearly impressed but also cautious. "That's bold."

I give a firm nod, holding his gaze. "If it means getting the deal done quickly, it's worth it."

"All right, I'll submit the offer and let you know their answer by the end of the week."

As soon as we got into the car, I sigh deeply, slumping back against the seat. "Thank god that's over."

Chase's voice is warm and sincere. "I thought you did great."

"Thanks," I reply, feeling a soft blush creep up my neck. "Anyway, I think that's the last of my errands. Do you want to head back to the hotel, or do you have anything else you need to do? I can be your chauffeur for the rest of the day since you've been so gracious to tag along with me."

Chase glances up through the windshield, his eyes scanning the area as if considering his next move. "Actually, yeah. I have one thing to do, and it's not far from here. You sure you've got time?"

I raise an eyebrow, smirking as I turn my attention back to him. "Oh, yeah. My only other plans were to accidentally run into a cute hockey player at my hotel bar and get him to flirt with me. But I suppose I can push that for you."

I watch his lips curl into a grin, his entire face lighting up with amusement. "Poor bastard."

It only takes five minutes to get to the address Chase has directed me to. After a final left turn, I pull up along the street in front of an incredible skyscraper building. Each floor seems to be nothing but floor-to-ceiling windows, the entire structure gleaming against the sky.

"Where are we?" I gasp, my eyes wide as I take in the stunning sight. I've lived in nice penthouses and million-dollar homes all my life, but this building is something else entirely.

"This is my apartment building," Chase says, his tone nonchalant but with a hint of pride.

"*What?*" I exclaim, unable to hide my shock. "You live here?" I shake my head in disbelief. "If I were you, I'd pay the contractors double just to get me back in here sooner."

He laughs, the sound rich and relaxed as he unbuckles his seatbelt and opens the door. "Eh, the hotel has everything I need," he says casually, as if the Four Seasons were just as comfortable as any penthouse.

Once again, I feel a flush of heat creep up my neck as I watch him move toward my door, his casual confidence making me feel like I should be more put-together.

"So why are we here?" I ask, stepping out of the car to catch up with him. "Is it close to being done?"

"Yeah, actually, it's almost ready," he answers, a touch of hesitation slipping into his voice. "I just need to pick the style and color for the new countertops and paint, and then they'll finish everything. I should be ready to move back in in a few weeks."

As he speaks, I notice the slight pause in his words, the faint hesitation that lingers, and I can't help but wonder what's holding him back.

Chase leads me inside, and I follow him through the glass doors of the building. The lobby is sleek and modern, filled with natural light streaming in from every direction. This place was designed to impress, with polished marble floors, high-end furniture, and art lining the walls. My heels click softly against the floor as I try to take in every detail of the space.

Chase smiles over his shoulder at me. "This place is insane, right?"

I nod, still in awe, and finally manage to speak. "Yeah, it's incredible. I don't think I've ever seen anything like it."

He laughs, leading me to the elevator. "Wait till you see the apartment. It's not as flashy as the lobby, but it's got an amazing view."

The elevator doors close with a soft hum, and we ascend quickly, the city skyline expanding around us as we rise. When the doors finally open, I step into the apartment, my eyes immediately drawn to the sweeping views of the city outside. The apartment is massive, with an open floor plan that seamlessly blends the kitchen, living, and dining spaces. The walls are bare, with only a few pieces of furniture placed here and there.

I walk in, my hand instinctively reaching for the railing along the balcony. The view is mesmerizing.

"You know I will never leave you alone now. I'm officially obsessed with your place."

He stands just behind me, his presence warm and solid. "Works for me."

We move to the kitchen area, where most of the renovation work is happening. There's a large, gleaming island in the middle of the room, with materials and samples spread out across the counter. A stack of design magazines sits beside a mood board that looks like a work of art in itself—colors, textures, and inspiration meticulously arranged and left by the designer he hired.

"So, what are we choosing today?" I ask, glancing at the samples spread out across the counter.

Chase picks up a set of paint swatches and hands them to me. "I'm leaning toward something warm for the walls. But I'm not sold yet."

I look through the colors, letting my fingers graze over the options. A warm neutral does seem like the right vibe for the space, but I'm drawn to something a little deeper—rich, earthy tones that still feel open and airy. "How about this?" I ask, pulling out a warm terracotta shade. "It's cozy but still light enough to feel open."

Chase looks over, his expression thoughtful. "Hmm. I like that. It's got some depth without making the place feel too small."

I smile, handing him the swatch. "It could be nice in the living area, but maybe something darker for the bedrooms?"

He nods in agreement. "I was thinking a forest green for the bedrooms. It has become my new favorite color recently."

"Yes, that's perfect."

As we continue discussing the options, the conversation becomes more natural, and I realize how easy it is to imagine myself here. The thought of choosing a space together, picking out the details, and making it *our* home feels right.

"Okay," I say after a while, finally deciding on a dark bedroom color. "I think we've got the paint colors sorted. Now what about the countertops?"

Chase pulls out a few samples, showing me a variety of options. There's marble, granite, and quartz, each with its own unique texture and look. I run my fingers over the smooth surfaces, my mind spinning with possibilities. I pick up a piece of quartz with subtle veins running through it, a soft white with hints of gray.

"This one," I say, turning it slowly in my hand. "It feels clean but still interesting. It'll contrast nicely with the terracotta on the walls."

Chase glances at the sample, then raises an eyebrow, a smile tugging at the corner of his mouth. "Hmm, I was actually leaning more toward the marble. It reminds me of the lobby, which you seemed to love."

I let out a soft laugh, shaking my head. "Well, well—our first disagreement on samples," I tease, glancing back at the other options. "Fine, you win, marble it is. You'll have to invite me over when everything is done so I can see it."

There's that flash of hesitation in his eyes again before the corners of his mouth flip up in a smile. "Of course."

CHAPTER SIXTEEN

Chase

It's been a week since Avery and I spent the day together—just running errands, living in the moment, and, despite everything, it felt effortless. If I thought I was a goner before, commit me now because Avery Keenen is the one for me. I'm sure of it. Every little thing about her—the way she smiles when she's thinking, the way she listens when I talk, the way she challenges me without even trying—has me completely wrapped up in her. There's no doubt in my mind. I've never felt this way about anyone, and I'm not about to let this slip through my fingers. Avery isn't just a fleeting moment, she's my best friend already and the one I want by my side.

And today brings us one day closer to making that a reality. The second charity event is today—the tailgate. The one thing missing from hockey is that we don't have tailgates like football, baseball, or even soccer. Sure, our fans show up, drink, and have a great time, but there's something about the energy of a tailgate. Some of my favorite non-playing sports memories are from those pre-game parties, where it's all about the community, the camaraderie, and the excitement of the game ahead. So when Avery suggested a hockey charity tailgate, I knew it would be something special.

You can feel the buzz in the air—it's the kind of event everyone is excited about. And with Avery leading the charge, I have no doubt it will be a huge success.

I know, even though I'm getting to the event over an hour early, Avery has been here since the crack of dawn, ensuring every detail is perfect. I expect to see a few food trucks, maybe some games, some kegs, and a few signs here and there. But when I pull into the parking lot, I'm completely taken aback. This isn't just a tailgate—it's a full-on carnival. The parking lot is transformed into something straight out of a dream. There's a Ferris wheel towering above the crowd, the colorful lights reflecting the morning sun, and a maze of tents and booths stretching farther than I can see. The air is filled with carnival music, and the sweet smell of popcorn and cotton candy drifts through the air. There are games and activities set up everywhere—giant Jenga, cornhole, a dunk tank, and even a mini petting zoo. It's not just a tailgate, it's an experience, and I can't help but smile.

That's Avery for you. She makes everything feel larger than life. She takes a simple idea and turns it into something unforgettable.

I'm quick out of the car, eager to find *my girl*. The player entrance is quiet this early, with only volunteers and the owners of various sponsor companies milling around. I offer polite nods as I weave through the rows, eyes scanning the crowd for Avery. It's been less than twenty-four hours since I last saw her but the pull to be near her feels like an unshakable magnet.

We've been keeping things strictly PG—sporadic kisses on the cheek, a casual brush of the hand—and it's been taking all of my willpower to keep it that way.

And just like that, she appears like a vision. Avery.

She's wearing tight, light-denim jeans and a Devils t-shirt, and her hair flows down in soft curls, the strands lifting slightly in the breeze as if she's a goddess making her way straight to me. In that moment, everything else fades away. The noise, the people, the event—it's all just background. My heart races as I watch her approach and feel my willpower snap. Every ounce of restraint I've been holding onto is gone instantly.

I step toward her, my legs moving faster than my thoughts, and before I can second-guess it, I pull her into a nearby tent away from the crowd. I quickly scan the area to make sure we're alone, and the second I'm sure we are, I close the space between us. My lips crash onto hers with no hesitation.

The moment our lips meet, the world shifts. She's soft and warm, and I don't think I've ever felt anything more perfect. My hands move to her waist instinctively, pulling her closer, and her body responds like it's always meant to be this way. I groan against her lips as she tilts her head, her mouth parting slightly, and I take it as an invitation to deepen the kiss. It's electric, everything I've been holding back, and I can't get enough.

After a few more moments, I reluctantly pull myself back and look at her. Her eyes are still closed, her lips swollen from the kiss, and she looks dazed, and it's the sexiest thing I've ever seen.

"What was that for?" she whispers, her voice soft.

I smile, still reeling from the kiss, and take a step back, letting out a breath I didn't realize I was holding. "This tailgate is amazing. I'm so proud of you," I say, my voice playful. "Plus, you look hot as hell, and I lost all self-control. So, yeah, guilty." I raise my arms in mock surrender, a grin tugging at my lips.

Her laughter fills the air, and I can't help but grin wider. She looks at me, her eyes still filled with warmth and amusement. "To hell with self-control."

***

The tailgate has been roaring for about an hour now and it's everything I imagined it would be—nothing short of a success. The place is packed; everywhere I look, there are people in Devil's gear, others playing games or jumping on rides. I can already tell Avery is going to blow her goals out of the water for this event

Still, I can't shake the nervous energy buzzing inside me. I keep checking my phone, a little anxious. I did something risky...something I'm starting to wonder if I overstepped. After our day together last week, I couldn't help but feel this urge to help Avery. I hate that she was carrying so much on her shoulders, and I thought, *Why not see if I can do something about it?*

My phone buzzes in my hand and I immediately swipe to check it.

> **Anthony:** I thought I was the only sibling of Avery's you knew.

> **Anthony:** Color me surprised when I run into Abigail and Adam on my way inside.

> **Anthony:** My sister is going to kill you.

I groan and look up just in time to see them walking through the gates. The trio of Avery's siblings is walking up, and she has no idea. I quickly look around to see if Avery is in sight, and when I don't see her anywhere, I start walking toward them.

"Anthony," I greet him, offering a firm handshake. "Hi, I'm Chase," I introduce myself to Adam and Abigail, keeping my tone warm and open.

Adam shakes my hand with a polite nod, but to my surprise, Abigail leans in for a quick hug.

"Thanks for inviting us," Adam says, his voice a bit awkward. I can sense the discomfort in their stance, as if they're unsure how to interact with each other or me. The urge to help her, to help them, flares up again.

"Avery is going to be excited to see you guys," I say with a smile. "She planned this whole thing, and I'm super proud of her." I glance between them, hoping my words will make them feel more at ease. If they're anything like their sister, they want to be close too, they just don't know how.

Just as we begin walking farther into the event, Avery rounds the corner, and the moment her eyes land on the four of us, she freezes, clearly taken aback. She just stands there, staring at us like she can't believe what she's seeing. Her expression shifts from surprise to something that might be disbelief, and I can almost see the gears turning in her head as she processes what's going on.

Slowly, Avery starts walking toward us, her eyes bouncing between each of us as if she's still trying to piece it all together. "Uh, what are you guys doing here?" she asks, her voice carrying a mix of confusion and surprise.

I'm about to speak, but Anthony beats me to it. "I called Abigail and Adam," he says, giving us all a quick glance. "I mentioned that we need to talk and this charity work thing you're running, and we wanted to support you." Anthony shoots me a subtle wink, and I smile back.

"You wanted to support...me?" she asks slowly, still in disbelief.

Abigail steps in before I can say anything, her voice soft but firm. "Yes, of course. Plus, apparently, we have to talk." She turns to Anthony, giving him a pointed look.

"Well, thank you for coming," Avery says, and I can tell she's genuinely happy.

Maybe I didn't overstep after all.

"Do you need to do anything for work, or do you have a minute to grab some food?" I ask, trying to gauge where her head is at. I don't want her to stress about work, but I also want her to spend time with her siblings if she can. "I can always handle anything you need if that's helpful."

Avery looks around for a second, then glances down at her iPad. "Uh, actually, I've got a bit. Do you guys want some food?" she asks.

Adam and Anthony both nod enthusiastically, and then in perfect sync, Abigail and Avery say at the same time, "I could go for a corndog."

Everyone freezes for a second, all four staring at each other in disbelief, like they can't quite believe they have something in common. I can't help but chuckle, shaking my head. "Let's go get the ladies some corndogs."

Anthony raises an eyebrow. "Who knew Ms. Abigail, the priss, would eat something as low-class as a corndog?" he teases, causing Abigail to roll her eyes.

"I could out-eat you any day, little brother," she shoots back, narrowing her eyes in a playful challenge.

Adam laughs, nudging Anthony. "Game on."

The past hour with the four Keenan siblings has been nothing short of heartwarming. It didn't take long for them to fall into an easy rhythm together, though there's still a hint of hesitancy here and there. I can tell they're all trying their best, and it makes me so happy Avery is finding a relationship with her brothers and sister.

At one point, Anthony and Avery started talking about their mom's journals and the building offer. There were a few lingering questions, but I could see their curiosity and openness.

We even ran into some of the guys by the cornhole setups. It was hard not to laugh when Billy shamelessly started flirting with Abigail, and even harder not to laugh when she flat-out turned him down without hesitation. She was cool about it, though, and Billy took it like a champ. The whole scene was hilarious, and it felt like we've all been friends for years. I glanced over at Avery during all of this, and my heart swelled at the sight of her bright eyes and smile.

I could spend the rest of my life watching this girl smile.

The day is going so perfectly, I should have known something or someone would throw it off, but fucking Campbell is not the thorn in my side I was anticipating. The five of us and Billy are sitting around a picnic table, laughing and joking, while Avery taps away on her iPad, going through updates for the event. The air is light, the mood perfect, but then I see him—Campbell—walking toward us. The second my eyes locked onto him, my gut clenches.

"Oh, what the fuck?" I mutter, standing up before I could stop myself.

Everyone at the table turns to look at me, and my eyes are already fixed on Avery, watching as she glances up and sees him too. Her expression shifts instantly from relaxed to tense. It's like she can feel the storm brewing even before it's arrived.

Campbell is only a few steps away now, and Avery immediately slides off the picnic table, moving as if instinctively to put some distance between herself and him. "Well, well, this is a rare sight," Campbell calls out, his voice dripping with that familiar smugness. "Who knew the Keenan kids just needed a couple of dead parents to get along?"

My blood boils. The words came out so easily like they mean nothing, but I know exactly how much weight they carry. I'm already taking a step toward him, every muscle in my body tense, ready to tear him apart, when Avery's hand shoots out and grips my forearm.

I stop, her touch grounding me just enough to keep me from charging at him. I can feel the tension between us, like a tug-of-war. Her siblings are starting to gather around us. Despite his dickhead comment, Campbell hasn't expected this—he hasn't expected them all to be here—and it's throwing him off.

Avery steps closer to me, her posture steady despite the tension in the air. "What do you want, Campbell?" she asks, her voice sharp.

Campbell's smirk falters for a second, but he quickly recovers. "Isn't it obvious?" he says with a shrug. "I'm here to support my wife."

My chest vibrates in anger and I take a step forward. This fucking guy is officially pissing me off. Avery grabs my forearm, keeping me from moving toward him. I take a step back, but she doesn't move her hand. Now her siblings are standing around us, and I swear Campbell is starting to feel intimidated.

"Seriously, man, what do you want? You can't be this bored?" Adam asks.

"I just wanted to let my wife know that we have a little bidding war going on now. I thought it would only be fair I let you know that you should find another building." He pauses, leaning in slightly toward Avery. "Or if you move back home, I'm sure we can negotiate a nice rental agreement."

Avery's eyes widen, the building she made a bid that was already over asking price—it should have been a done deal, and now this fucking guy is outbidding her.

I feel the blood pumping through my veins and my fists are clenched to the side.

"That's extortion, dumbass," Abigail responds. "Do you really think I won't come for you if you try and screw us over?"

"Too late. Bids are already in." He smirks. "Are you sure you don't want to come home, honey?" he asks, looking at Avery, but she stays silent.

"You're starting to piss me off, Cam. Back off," Anthony warns.

"A little late to come play the protective older brother act, don't you think?" he says to Anthony and then turns his attention back to Avs, taking a small step toward her. "Come on, Av, they were never your family. You know th—"

He doesn't get to finish his sentence before Anthony knocks him out cold.

Chapter Seventeen

Avery

Having siblings is fun—if I'd known they were out there punching toxic ex-husbands, I'd have made more of an effort to stay close over the years. *Just kidding...mostly.*

Campbell stumbles to his feet, blood dripping from his split lip.

"Campbell, you need to go. Now." My voice is firm and steady.

His eyes narrow, and he sneers, "We'll talk."

Abigail steps in, her voice is cold and decisive. "No, you won't. Any further communication will go through her lawyer—me." She pauses, letting her words sink in. "I'd suggest you retract your offer within the next twenty-four hours, or I promise you will regret it."

He doesn't answer—just glares at us, his pride bruised as much as his face. Without another word, he stumbles off, leaving us in tense silence.

I exhale slowly, my eyes flicking over to the people around me and finally landing on my brother. "You okay?" I ask.

"Avs, I'm fine," Anthony says with a reassuring grin. "I fight for a living."

I shrug, the words a little hollow in my head. He's right. Still, my mind is spinning, processing everything that just happened. But my thoughts are interrupted when Adam pulls out his phone, his expression turning serious. A few seconds later, he looks up, his voice tight. "I've been called into the hospital. I have to go."

Without warning, he steps forward, pulling me into a hug. For a moment, I freeze in surprise, but then I lean into it, feeling the warmth of his support. "Thank you for coming," I whisper.

Abigail clears her throat, gesturing toward herself and Anthony. It's a subtle cue that it's time for them to leave too. "We should head out. But call me tomorrow and let's talk, okay?"

"Yeah," I reply softly. "I'll call you."

After we exchange quick goodbyes, I turn to Chase. He's already watching me, his expression filled with concern.

I offer him a small, reassuring smile. "I'm okay."

His brow furrows, his doubt lingering in his voice. "Are you sure?"

I glance around, my eyes landing on one of the rented rides—the Gravitron. It looks like a spaceship, sleek and metallic, designed to spin and press you against the walls, simulating a lack of gravity. When I arrived this morning, it was the one hiccup in an otherwise flawless event—Campbell aside. The ride wouldn't work, and by the time they figured it out, it was too late to get it out of the lot. So now it sits there, abandoned, taking up space, a reminder of the things that went wrong today.

I squeeze Chase's hand and pull him toward the ride. It's tucked away in a quiet corner, secluded from the rest of the commotion. A perfect spot for just the two of us. Exactly what I need right now.

I pull us inside and guide Chase into the chair meant for the operator in the middle of the ride. Without thinking twice, I climb on top of him, my legs straddling his as I throw my arms around his neck.

"Hi," I breathe out.

"Hi," he says, his voice soft as his hands gently move up to push my hair out of my face. "Are you sure you're okay?"

I feel his fingers linger at my temple, the warmth of his touch sending shivers down my body. I don't answer right away. Instead, I lean in, closing the small space between us, and kiss him, slow and deep, letting the world outside fade into nothing.

Pulling away, I look into his eyes, my breath shaky but steady. "Yes." I lean in again, this time more urgently, but then I pull back again. "You called my brother?"

His gaze softens, a flicker of uncertainty crossing his face. He pulls back slightly, his voice unsure. "Are you mad?"

I meet his eyes, the vulnerability in his question making my heart tighten. "No, in fact, I think it's about to get you very lucky."

I don't know what I'm doing. I know this is a bad idea—I've told myself a thousand times that I need to keep my distance. And yet, every time I'm near him, he has me not caring about any of it. So, fully aware of the hypocrisy, I dip my head and connect my lips with his.

My mouth moves over his eagerly. Chase's hands still in my hair, pull slightly, not enough to hurt, but enough to send a jolt through my body. He tastes like funnel cake and Diet Coke, and it's addicting. My tongue sweeps his lips, desperate to get more of a taste.

"Avery," Chase mumbles against my lips.

"Chase," I mimic.

"If you think the first time we have sex is going to be in a broken fair ride, you're sadly mistaken." His words sound mumbled since we are still kissing as he tries to say them.

I pull back slightly, smirking. "You're going to turn down eager and willing me?" I joke.

"I will haul your sexy ass back to the hotel right now, but when we have sex for the first time, I want to take my time with you, baby."

I get what he's saying, and part of me wants that too, but also, the bigger part of me wants him right now.

"I want you so bad," I mumble in his ear, my tongue doing circles on his earlobe, causing his hips to thrust into my core. "Chase," I say, grabbing his face between my hands. "I want you now, you don't need to protect me. I want the dirty hot sex in the Gravitron." I laugh. "Do you?"

Chase blows a low whistle. "Of course, I do."

Within seconds, he rips my shirt off and I do the same to him, his bare chest revealed. He's cut like a diamond, and my hands run down his rough edges, leaving me breathless, and arousal is spreading deep in my core.

His mouth stays locked to mine as one hand cups my breast, making me grind down into him even harder. My pulse goes haywire while he slightly moves me up to pull down my pants. I stand quickly, pulling my pants down, as he raises his hips and tugs his down as well.

"You sure no one's coming in here?" he asks as we're in the frenzy of removing the remaining clothes. Getting fully naked to have sex in here is a…choice…but I want all of him, so to the hell with consequences.

"Nope, really have no clue."

Chase laughs, pulling me back into him. When my wet heat makes contact with his hard dick, a deep husky moan slips from his mouth and my body is sent into overdrive. I slowly rub up and down, teasing him while getting wetter by the second. His fingers move down my body until they find my clit. He rubs tiny circles around my sensitive skin before sliding two fingers in me. The orgasm is immediate and needy. I was desperate for his touch, and as soon as his fingers were inside me, my body pulsated around him.

He groans, pulling out slowly. "Are you ready, baby?"

I am. I need this. I need him.

"Yes." I nod, breathless and needy. I lower myself slowly, inch by inch, feeling the amazing stretching sensation the whole way down, and suddenly I'm full. My inner muscles wrap around him, his groan rings through my body,

"Fuck, baby." Chase's fingers dig into my hips, keeping me in place. "Fuck. Okay, I just needed a second."

He releases me slightly, and I lift myself and slam down so hard and deep we both groan in pleasure. Now it's a frenzy—our bodies are crushed together, he's leaving wet, sloppy kisses down my neck, and my body is moving up and down, catching the third orgasm within minutes.

One of the first nights we played two truths and a lie, I told him I'm on birth control and also hate sex with condoms. Now I remember why—his bare length inside me sends ripples of intense pleasure through me. My pussy contracts, pulsating around his long length, and his lips connect with mine, letting me moan into his mouth. As soon as my orgasm finishes, I feel his dick pulsate, and it's such an arousal that a fourth orgasm rides around me and I lose my breath.

After a few seconds, I pull myself off him, and we quickly get dressed. As I get ready to start walking toward the door, he grabs my arm and pulls me into him, kissing me long and slow.

"You're fucking beautiful, Avery."

***

Finally collapsing into the softness of my hotel bed after what will undoubtedly go down as the longest day of my life feels like a dream. The mattress is heaven, and I can already tell I will miss it when I eventually leave. It's so ridiculously comfortable I might just want to take it with me. I should be thinking about finding a more permanent place than the Four Seasons, but that's a problem for a different day. My brain can't seem to process anything other than the multiple orgasms Chase gave me on an amusement park ride and how good this bed feels now.

As much as my body craves sleep, my mind is too restless to shut off anytime soon. After a few moments of letting my body sink into the mattress, I reluctantly pull myself up. I change into comfy sweats, feeling the soft fabric settle around me, and gather my hair into a messy bun on top of my head.

Chase practically begged to come back to my room tonight, but after everything that happened today, it made more, I don't know, *sense* to be alone. Even though now, I can't stop wishing I'd agreed to be with him.

I glance at my mom's journals on the desk, their worn covers staring back at me. It feels like forever since I last picked them up, even though it's only been a few days. Anthony mentioned he read through the first journal, the one from her pregnancy with Abigail, and that he'd already passed it to her. He hasn't started the one about himself yet. I get it. Knowing the heartbreak you're about to dive into before you even open the pages—that would be scary for anyone.

I reach for the next journal in the stack, my fingers brushing lightly over the cover. My heart begins to race, the familiar anxiety creeping up my throat. The last journal I read was filled with her depression, her sense of hopelessness thick in every word. Knowing she gets pregnant again, I don't know what to expect when I open this journal.

I take a deep breath before flipping open the pages and diving in.

January 1st, 1994

It's a new year, and like I promised myself, I think we're going to find our way back. Daniel even scheduled us to see a couple's therapist he said a coworker recommended.

Daniel seems happier—he got a job promotion and is making more money than we could have dreamed about. He says it's just the beginning. I brought up the idea of the library/speakeasy last night, but it was somewhat brushed off. To be fair, it was New Year's Eve, and he'd been drinking. I'll bring it up again tomorrow.

Here's to 1994.

January 15th, 1994

We went to our first couples' therapy session today. It was awful. The therapist was thin, blonde, and barely looked at me the whole time. She wore a tight dress and eight-inch heels, while I showed up in worn jeans and a shirt with dried spit-up on it. She looked like a far better fit for Daniel than me. Her name is Cindy, and I know I shouldn't be mean, but I don't like her or her name.

Whenever I brought something up, she told me not to worry about it and reminded me how lucky I am to be home with my children. She even encouraged us to try for another, which I don't understand. I feel like I should be focusing on my current kids—and maybe myself—but Daniel jumped on the idea so quickly. Maybe I'm just stuck in my own head?

I don't know. I need more time to think.

January 22, 1994

We went back for our second therapy session, and I hated it just as much as the first. Cindy spent most of the time pushing the idea of having another baby, and when I tried to steer the conversation to the business, I swear I saw smoke coming out of Daniel's ears. I will have some making up to do tonight.

February 10th, 1994

Daniel got what he wanted. I'm pregnant. And he told me, in no uncertain terms, that the library idea is not going to happen. He doesn't believe in it—and he never did.

I'm starting to think Daniel isn't someone I can rely on. I can't leave—not with two toddlers and being pregnant. But maybe I can figure out a way to live with him, but without him.

Maybe 1994 is not my year.

February 14, 1994

Valentine's Day. Another day I used to care about, but now it's just another date on the calendar. Daniel took me out for dinner and we had a nice time—well, as nice as we could manage. There was no spark. There was no connection, and I don't know if it's him or if it's me.

I still love him. I do. I even saw the excitement on Daniel's face when I told him I was pregnant, and he even agreed to find a new therapist who's not Cindy. But I'm afraid that the distance between us is too much now. The space between us feels wider than ever.

Maybe it's me. Maybe I'm the problem.

March 10, 1994

It's been two years since we first discussed the restaurant idea and a month since he told me it will never happen. The dream still lingers, but there's no energy behind it. Not anymore. Daniel's too focused on work, and I'm too...lost to think clearly.

I feel like I'm suffocating. The hotel project is moving forward, and Daniel seems completely consumed by it. I can't blame him. Maybe we both need something to hold on to, but I miss the excitement we used to have together.

I need to do something. I need to retake control because Abigail and Adam run the show at home. I'm caving to anything they want. Daniel controls the finances and everything else, and I control...nothing.

I close the journal. Two glasses of wine and an hour of reading later, my brain is still spinning. The more I learn about my mother, the less I feel like I know. I need a new distraction—the numbers from today's event won't be ready until tomorrow. I glance at the clock: 11:08 p.m.

I know what will make me sleep—a hot, six-two hockey player with his arms wrapped around me. I glance at my phone, debating texting Chase.

"Fuck it," I mutter to myself, grabbing my phone and keys and heading out the door instead. "You got this, Avery," I whisper, pumping myself up as I approach the elevator.

But as soon as I step in and the doors close behind me, I realize I'm still in a messy bun and sweats. I almost turn around, but the elevator doors open onto his floor just as I do.

"Well...I guess, fuck it again," I mutter, shaking my head as I head for his door.

I knock gently on the door twice, the sound soft but deliberate. My heart pounds in my chest as I place my arm by my side, willing my nerves to settle.

"You got this," I whisper to myself one more time as a final pep talk.

As I draw a steadying breath, the door swings open and Chase stands in the doorway. He's dressed in nothing but a pair of black sweats, his sculpted torso bare, his hair still wet and messy from a recent shower, adding to his raw, effortless appeal that only makes my pulse race faster.

"I swear to God, Chase, you're too hot for your own good." I laugh, the words slipping out with playful disbelief. "If it weren't for the multiple orgasms not even six hours ago, I'd be jumping you right now."

He leans against the door frame, his posture relaxed but confident. "You're great for a man's ego, baby," he replies, his smile effortless, immediately calming all my nerves.

I give a small, hesitant smile. "Is it okay that I'm here?"

"You never have to ask, Avs. Of course, it's okay," he says, taking a step back. He opens the door wider and invites me into his room.

I look around, taking in his room, which is nearly identical to mine—same layout, same furniture. "After all this time, I don't think I've ever been in your room," I say, glancing over the familiar chaos.

Chase flashes a grin, leaning against the doorframe. "I'm glad you finally made it. Couldn't stay away?"

I roll my eyes, trying to hide a smile. "Yeah," I admit, shrugging. "But don't get too excited. It's probably just a chemical thing—like I said, multiple orgasms"

He bursts out laughing. "Like I said, good for the ego, baby."

He walks over to his bed, casually climbing in and pulling the covers up, making himself comfortable. I stand there, unsure of what to do next.

"What are you doing?" I ask, my eyes fixed on him.

"What are you doing?" he shoots back with a mischievous grin.

"I don't know…I just came because…" I hesitate, the truth slowly spilling out. "I don't know, okay? I couldn't sleep and I just wanted to see you."

Chase's eyes soften as he looks up at me from under the covers, and his voice warms. "I missed you too, beautiful."

CHAPTER EIGHTEEN

Chase

Waking up with my arms wrapped around Avery is as close to perfection as I'll ever get. Her body fits against mine as effortlessly as two pieces of a puzzle coming together. The warmth of her body pressed against me has me almost forgetting about the outside world—about everything that happened yesterday.

The cocky, alpha part of me is itching to remind her that she technically gave in and lost the bet, and it's time we stop pretending this isn't a thing. Part of me wants to push for more, to seize the moment and make her mine. But then there's the more rational part of me that knows even though Avery is a true goddess, the woman is as skittish as Bambi in the woods. If I push too hard or rush her before she's ready I'll only scare her away, and I can't let that happen. This—*us*—it's too important to mess up.

I press my lips gently to her shoulder blade, savoring the warmth of her skin beneath me. I know the reality of the day is waiting just around the corner. Workouts start in less than an hour, and I will be late if I don't pull myself away from her soon.

Avery stirs beneath me, the soft movement pulling me back into her, and I lean in to kiss her again, this time on her temple.

"Shh," I whisper against her ear, my voice low. "I have to go to the arena, but it's still early...keep sleeping."

I know it's a fool's request. The moment I slip out the door, she'll wake up and start her day, but the thought of Avery curled up in my bed, waiting for me to come back, is too perfect not to try.

"Mmm," she hums softly as she flips over to face me, her eyes still heavy with sleep but full of warmth. "Will you hold it against me if I say I don't want you to go?" She tightens her arms around me, and I swear my heart nearly combusts.

I gently lift her chin, my thumb grazing her skin, and press my lips to hers. My voice is low as I murmur, "I'll call in sick." The words come out with a smile, and she laughs softly.

"I don't think they'll believe you," she teases. "Since they all saw you yesterday and everything."

"I'll call in dead," I counter with a smirk.

She laughs again, and I pull her back into me, claiming her mouth with mine once more, letting the moment stretch between us. Her hand rests lightly on my chest, her fingers tracing small, slow circles.

"I have to leave in an hour," she says with a sigh. "So I'd be ditching you if you didn't ditch me first."

"Ugh." I groan dramatically, rolling onto my back and staring at the ceiling. "Fine, I'll leave the beautiful woman in my bed. Only because she's making me," I add, sarcasm dripping from every word.

She moves quickly as she rolls on top of me and straddles me. "I know, I know, I'm terrible," she says, her voice teasing, her eyes sparkling with mischief. "But maybe I can make it up to you...dinner tonight?"

"Really?" I reply, looking up at her, unable to hide the hint of a smile forming on my lips.

She leans down, her lips brushing softly against mine as she whispers, "Yes."

I pull back just enough to meet her gaze, my heart racing. "It's a date."

***

Weights crash against the floor with a sharp, metallic clang, blending with the high-pitched squeak of sneakers slicing across polished wood—the air hums with energy and unspoken competition. Riley is already in the corner, his posture loose but alert, a cocky grin tugging at his lips as he flips a medicine ball from hand to hand with effortless precision, like it's just an extension of him. Jamie stands at the bench press, spotting Billy who's pushing out his last few reps.

"You're slacking, Matthews," Riley says, his voice laced with mock disdain as I approach. "What's the matter? Finally realized you're no match for me?" He tosses the medicine ball in my direction, and I catch it instinctively, the impact reverberating through my arms.

"Slacking? You wish," I shoot back, tossing the ball harder than necessary.

Riley catches it with a grunt, laughing.

"Don't let him get to you," Jamie chimes in, stepping back as Billy racks the bar with a loud clang. "Riley's just bitter because he lost our bet yesterday and got put on blast right in front of our parents."

"Oh, come on," Riley protests, his grin widening. "That call was garbage, and you know it. Plus, you can try all you want, Jamie, I'll always be the favorite."

"Excuses, excuses," Billy says, wiping sweat off his forehead. He grabs a water bottle and takes a long swig before adding, "Maybe if you spent less time talking and more time training, you'd actually win your family Monopoly tournament for once."

"I'll remember that next time I'm carrying the team, and you're on the sidelines playing Monopoly Go on your phone," Riley shoots back, and we all laugh.

It's the kind of easy banter that only comes from spending countless hours together, both on and off the ice. When I met these guys, they already had a dynamic—Jamie and Riley, of course, because they're brothers, but Billy too, and somehow they let me in. It's a camaraderie forged in late-night road trips, relentless drills at dawn, and post-game celebrations where victories are shared and defeats are mourned together. Moments like Jamie standing up for Riley in a heated argument with a ref or Billy's endless knack for finding the perfect quip to break the tension—they are my family.

As the laughter fades, Jamie nudges me with his elbow, a sly smirk tugging at the corner of his mouth. "So, what's the deal with you and Avery? Word is, her ex showed up yesterday, and her brother decked him in front of everyone."

"I was there," Billy cuts in, pointing a thumb toward me. "And if her brother hadn't handled it, this guy was about ten seconds away from doing the honors himself."

My jaw tightens at the memory. The surge of anger I'd felt toward Campbell still simmering under the surface.

"Yeah, Campbell's a piece of shit," I say flatly, the edge in my tone unmistakable. "Rich, alpha-douchebag type who thinks he owns Avery. If Abigail doesn't get him to back off soon, I'm stepping in. He's not going to keep walking all over her."

"Dude," Jamie interjects, his voice laced with concern. "Please don't go getting yourself kicked off the team right before the season starts. Especially not over some girl."

"Fuck off," I snap, turning to glare at him. "She's not just some girl."

Jamie immediately throws up his hands in surrender, his expression softening. "Easy, man. I didn't mean it like that. I like Avery—she's great. But you've got to admit, she's dealing with some heavy stuff right now. I just don't want you getting caught in the crossfire."

I give him a curt nod, my lips pressed into a thin line. He means well, I know that, but his advice isn't what I need right now. What I want is their support. I'm going to give this thing with Avery a shot if she'll let me.

Jamie must pick up on my desire to move on because he quickly shifts his attention to Billy, a mischievous glint in his eye.

"Speaking of the Keenan sisters..." Jamie starts, his voice brimming with mock enthusiasm. "I heard Billy boy here got shot down hard by the older one."

Billy groans, his head dropping back as if the ceiling might save him from the teasing. "Oh, fuck off, Jamie," he retorts, his tone exasperated but his cheeks flushing all the same.

Jamie chuckles, undeterred. "Come on, spill it. What happened? Did she laugh in your face, or was it one of those polite-but-devastating letdowns?"

Billy swipes at Jamie with a towel, missing entirely, and we all dissolve into laughter again, the gym echoing with the sound.

***

After the talk with the guys, I don't find myself heading back to the hotel to get ready for dinner with Avery. Instead, I find my hands gripping the steering wheel, taking me in a completely different direction—toward her ex-husband.

I don't have a plan, but I have the concept of what I want to happen—now, it's to see if I can make it a reality versus the alternative, which would end in me in prison for first-degree murder.

Avery has mentioned where Campbell works a couple of times, so tracking down his office building isn't difficult. I considered calling ahead to make an appointment, but I have a feeling he is cowardly enough to bail before I even get there. No, a surprise visit is the best way to handle him.

I park right on the street in front of his building, taking a deep breath before heading toward the entrance. My footsteps are deliberate as I walk past the glass doors and toward the receptionist's desk.

"Hi, I'm here to see Campbell Ryan," I say, my voice confident.

The receptionist looks up from her screen, her eyes flicking to mine, and I see the recognition flicker across her face. A smile slowly spreads on her lips. "You're Chase Matthews. Wow, I'm a huge fan. Yes, let me get you checked in."

I flash her a quick smile. "Thank you."

She types away at her computer, the soft click of keys filling the brief silence, but then her face shifts. A frown tugs at the corners of her lips as she looks back at me. "I'm sorry, Mr. Matthews, but I don't see you on Mr. Ryan's calendar."

My mind races for a way around this. "Yes, I know," I say smoothly, not missing a beat. "I'm actually here because Campbell won season tickets from a charity event he attended yesterday, and I want to deliver them personally."

I let the words hang in the air, watching her reaction closely.

She hesitates for a moment, her fingers still on the keyboard, and then her face brightens into another smile. "Season tickets? That's wonderful! I'm sure he'll be so excited."

I nod. "I hope so. Can I go ahead and head back?" I gesture toward the double glass doors that lead into the inner offices.

"Here, let me walk you back!" she says, her voice suddenly warmer, almost eager, as she rounds the desk and starts toward the hallway.

I follow her as we pass through the quiet, sterile corridors, the soft hum of office equipment and muted voices filling the air. She leads me toward a door at the far end, then pauses to knock lightly before opening it.

"Mr. Ryan?" she calls into the office, her voice chipper. "Chase Matthews is here to deliver the season tickets."

"Thanks, Deb." Campbell nods, barely sparing a glance at the receptionist as she exits. "Close the door on your way out."

Deb doesn't hesitate, stepping out of the office without a word. The soft click of the door closing echoes through the room, but neither of us look away. It's like a silent standoff, the air thick with unspoken history between us.

Campbell's gaze sharpens, his jaw tightens. "What are you doing here?"

"I'm here to talk about Avery."

His eyes narrow, and his lips curl into a smirk. "And what exactly about my wife would you like to talk about?"

My hands instinctively ball into fists. I force myself to breathe, to keep my temper in check. He wants a reaction—he's trying to bait me to see how far he can push. The problem is, standing here in front of him, looking at his smug face and his douchey suit, I'm starting to feel like he might get what he wants.

"Come on, man, you're getting pathetic. She doesn't want to be with you—let her go and stop trying to fuck with her."

Campbell laughs, shaking his head, and he rounds the desk to stand at its side. " Let me get this straight. You've known Avery for what, a month, give or take? And you think you know her? I've known this girl my whole life. I think you need to stay in your lane. You think your meathead tactics scare me? You have no idea what you're dealing with."

I take a step forward, grabbing Campbell by the collar of his suit and shoving him back into the wall. "Here's what I do know. In the time I have known her, all she has wanted is to reconnect with her siblings and find some closure after her mom's death. If you loved her, you would want that for her, whether she wants to be with you or not, but all you are doing is trying to sabotage her. And I'm telling you, Campbell, if you don't sign the divorce papers and retract your bid today, I don't care about my hockey contract or whatever you think you can do to me. I will end you."

He takes his hands and pushes me off him. I let go willingly but don't move.

"Get off me, you fucking low-life criminal." He wipes his hands down his front, straightening out his suit. "Even if I drop the bid and sign the divorce papers, she'll never be yours. That bitch is just like her siblings and her mother—cold, rigid, incapable of love—she'll leave you high and dry. And when it happens she'll stumble back to me, because, at the end of the day, I know who she is."

I take a step, ready to bash his face in, but somehow I find the strength to contain myself. "You know what? You're not worth it because it's clear you know nothing about that girl. Avery gives as much love as she gets. So, yeah, if you're a condescending, cold-hearted, dick-head who fumbled the best woman he will ever get—yeah, she may be a little closed-off. But if you treat her how she deserves and give her the freedom to be who she wants to be, she loves harder than anyone I've ever seen."

I walk toward the door but turn around at the last second. "Don't make me come back here, Campbell. Back off."

CHAPTER NINETEEN

Avery

It's just after seven when Chase steps into the hotel bar, a scowl etched across his face. In all the time we've spent together, living in this hotel, I realize I've never seen him this angry before—and now that I have, I don't like it.

"Chase!" I shout across the room, drawing his attention to me. The moment his eyes meet mine, his tense expression softens, and a wave of relief washes over me. He quickly approaches me and gives me a quick peck on the cheek.

"Are you okay?" I ask as he sits on the bar stool next to me.

"Yeah, rough day, but better now that I'm with you," he replies, his voice soft as he lifts his hand, his fingers brushing gently against my skin as he tucks a stray lock of hair behind my ear.

The simple touch sends a shiver down my spine, and for a moment, I'm tempted to lean in for a kiss. But I hold back. Chase is perfect—attentive, supportive, and easily the most beautiful man I've ever seen. Yet, I'm still hesitant to take that step, and I can't quite figure out why.

"How was your day?" Chase asks.

Just as I'm about to answer, my phone buzzes on the bar in front of me, the screen lighting up with Abigail's name.

"Sorry, can you give me a minute?" I say, already reaching for the phone.

He nods. "Of course." He turns away to wave Steven down at the bar.

"Hey, Abs, what's up?" I answer, trying to hide the flicker of nerves, not used to my sister calling me, and realizing that for the first time in probably ever, I don't call her by her full name.

"Hey," she replies, her tone a little hesitant. "So, I have good news and bad news. Which would you like to hear first?"

"Bad news, of course," I answer automatically.

"Okay, so the good news is," she begins, completely ignoring my request, "Campbell backed out of his bid, so the building is officially ours. Well, yours and Anthony's, until we figure out all the paperwork. But you did it, Avery. The building is ours."

I let out a breath I didn't even realize I'd been holding. Campbell backed out. The building is ours. We really did it. The enormity of the moment hits me, and instinctively I reach for Chase's hand, squeezing it tightly.

"We got the building," I mouth quickly, my eyes wide with excitement, before turning my attention back to my sister.

"Okay, so what's the bad news?" I ask, my voice low but still filled with that lingering rush knowing I'm making my mom's dream a reality.

Abigail hesitates for a second, then sighs. "Well, Campbell got around to backing out of the bid, but he hasn't gotten around to signing any divorce papers yet."

I roll my eyes. "Yeah, well, we knew he wouldn't make it that simple," I mumble under my breath. "But it's a step in the right direction. He'll sign, he just needs to get over his bruised ego."

I feel Chase's gaze on me as I talk to Abigail, but when I glance at him, his expression is unreadable.

"Well, while you live in that nice little fairytale," Abigail says with a hint of sarcasm, "I'm going the realistic route. I've got a call scheduled with his lawyer tomorrow. I will figure out what the hold-up is and get this done. With the business, we need you two divorced before that place is up and running."

I nod, knowing she's right. "Let me know how it goes," I reply, my tone more serious now.

"I will," she agrees. "Also, I sent a calendar invite for the four of us to Zoom tomorrow and talk about next steps with the business now that the building is ours."

I raise an eyebrow, trying to hide a smile, even though she can't see me. "How official."

"You're welcome," Abigail sings in that way that makes me laugh, her personality breaking through.

"I'll talk to you tomorrow." I laugh.

I set my phone down and glance at Chase, his face still emotionless.

"He still hasn't signed the divorce papers?" His voice is cold, cutting through the room, and I hate how it makes me instinctively want to raise all my walls.

"Not yet," I admit, forcing a shaky laugh. "But he did back out of the bid for the building, so...baby steps, right?"

"Yeah," he says, his nod slow and deliberate. "Baby steps."

"Are you sure you're okay?" I ask softly, resting my hand gently on his arm.

"I'm okay," he replies, but I can't tell if he's trying to convince me or himself.

I glance at Chase, the tension still visible in the tight set of his jaw and the way his fingers tap an uneven rhythm against the bar top. He's trying to play it cool, but I can see the storm brewing behind his eyes.

"Chase," I say softly, leaning closer. "Let's not do this tonight."

His eyes snap to mine, confusion flickering across his face. "Do what?"

"Talk about Campbell. Or the divorce. Or anything that has to do with him," I say, my voice steady but gentle. "I don't want him taking up space here. Not with you."

The corners of his mouth tug upward slightly, and he lets out a breath, some of the tension leaving his shoulders. "You're right. I don't want to give that guy any more of our time."

"Good," I reply, smiling. "Because I'm starving, and I'd much rather spend the night talking about anything else. Like, why do you look so good even after a rough day?"

Chase's lips curve into a full smile now, the kind that makes my stomach do a little flip. "I don't know," he says, leaning closer. "Maybe it's because I was motivated, knowing I'd be seeing you tonight."

I laugh, rolling my eyes. "Smooth."

"Was it?" he teases, signaling Steven for a menu. "I thought it was just honest."

We quickly order, and as we wait for our food the conversation shifts to lighter topics—the ridiculous playlist the gym had on this morning, Riley getting smacked in the face by a medicine ball, my Pinterest inspiration board for the business. All effortless, easy, and I know I'm in trouble.

***

What originally starts as a Zoom call becomes an in-person meeting at the building. Less than an hour after hanging up with Abigail last night, Anthony and I had paperwork in our inboxes to sign and send back, and by this morning the keys were ours. Abigail made sure everything moved quickly to avoid any setbacks in case Campbell decided to change his mind again.

So now, at 8 a.m., I'm making my way to the East Side.

When I arrive and step inside, I find Abigail and Anthony already there. Abigail stands with her arms crossed, assessing the room like it's a court case to win, while An-thony lazily leans against a column, clearly unimpressed.

"So, how does it look?" I ask, my voice bubbling with excitement.

"Dirty," she says dryly, a smirk tugging at her lips.

"It looks good," Anthony adds, glancing around. "But honestly, Avs, I feel like you can see Mom's vision much better than we can."

The door creaks, pulling all three of our attention to-ward it as Adam walks in. He's dressed in black sweat-pants and a matching hoodie, his hair still damp from what I assume was a rushed shower.

"Sorry," he mutters, striding toward us. "Surgery ran long." He pauses, looking around the space, his eyes taking in every inch of the building. "So this piece of shit is ours, huh?"

I roll my eyes. "Nice, Adam. Really."

He raises his hands in mock surrender. "Kidding," he says, grinning. "Kind of."

"So, step one," Abigail starts, shifting into boss mode, "we need to get this place cleaned up, the trash out, and then bring in some experts to make sure the building, electrical, and all that stuff is good to go. Once we've got the green light and get insurance secured, we'll move on from there."

"Are we starting right now?" I ask, scanning the space around us.

Abigail nods. "Yes. We're all free today, which is rare, and why I changed it from Zoom to in-person and forced the old owner to give me the keys early. So we're going to clean and multitask. While we're at it, we can figure out how we want to move forward with everything and who can actually do what.

Adam and Anthony both bend down, grabbing rolls of trash bags. They rip off a stack and hand it to us without hesitation.

"Let's get to work," Adam says.

The cleaning quickly becomes a mix of awkwardness and chaos. None of us are exceptionally comfortable working together or doing manual labor in this way, and it shows.

Adam tries to tackle the piles of trash by the far wall, but he pushes half of it to the floor and reaches for a bag. It lands with a loud thud. He pauses, looks at it, and sighs. "Well, that was productive," he mutters, throwing the trash into the bag exaggeratedly.

Anthony's been stuck with cleaning the windows, but it's clear that he has no idea what he's doing. He keeps wiping them in circles, leaving more streaks than when he started. After a few attempts, he stares at the glass and then turns to Abigail. "Is this...better? Or is it worse?"

Abigail steps over and inspects his work, her lips curling into a tiny smirk. "It's definitely...worse."

I can't help but laugh, but as soon as I do, I get distracted and accidentally knock over an old bucket and it spills across the floor, scattering dust and debris everywhere.

Meanwhile, Abigail is in full-on boss mode, pulling us back on track. "All right," she says, eyeing us as we try to salvage the mess. "I think we've got the cleaning covered...mostly. Let's talk business."

We gather around, sitting on some of the old furniture that's still in the building.

"So, we've got the concept nailed down—based on Mom's journals and some general research," she says, tapping her fingers on the table. "But how do we make this work? How's this thing going to run? We all have full-time jobs."

"I think the day-to-day's going to be key," I say, leaning back in my chair. "We need someone who will be here a lot, overseeing everything, managing staff, dealing with customers."

Anthony pipes up. "And handling all the weird, drunk people who come at night."

"Exactly. And since I got the ball rolling on this, I'll do it. My job with the Devils is over in three weeks, and then I can make this my top focus and can handle the day-to-day at the start."

Adam raises an eyebrow. "So you want to be the one dealing with all the headaches? All the...*difficult* people?"

I roll my eyes, grinning. "You're welcome to step in anytime, Adam. If you want the job, you're more than welcome to take it."

Before Adam can respond, Anthony cuts in. "Once we get this place up and running, I can coordinate security. Plenty of guys I know are looking for extra work."

Abigail smiles, clearly pleased with how things are shaping up. "All right, so we've got our GM and security. Now we need a team to get this place up and running."

Adam starts rifling through a pile of papers. "I'll be the resident wine expert. No one's more qualified than me when it comes to drinking it. Also, add me to the list for supplying the books—might as well be the go-to guy for both."

"And I'll handle everything from a business setup and legal perspective," Abigail chimes in, giving the room a quick once-over. "But I think we've got a solid start here. Let's finish cleaning this place up."

I glance at the others and then at the mess we've created, shaking my head. "I can't believe we're doing this..." I pause for a moment. "Together."

Anthony claps me on the shoulder, giving it a firm squeeze. "We're doing it," he says, a smirk tugging at his lips.

Tears well up in my eyes, but I quickly laugh, shaking them away. "All right, so...what about a name?"

"She didn't have one?" Adam asks, turning toward me.

"No, not that I've found yet," I admit with a shrug.

"Hmm. How about *Books and Bourbon*?" Anthony suggests, his lips curving into a playful grin.

Abigail immediately shakes her head. "A little too on the nose, don't you think? And what's with the bourbon? I thought Mom wanted wine."

"She definitely talked about wine," I agree.

Anthony crosses his arms, unwavering. "No way I'm doing this without bourbon."

"Same," Adam chimes in.

Abigail sighs, tilting her head. "All right, what about...the *Winebrary*?"

"Isn't that already a thing?" I ask, wrinkling my nose.

A name suddenly pops into my head, and before I can overthink it, I blurt out, "What about *Binds and Barrels*?"

Abigail's eyes light up. "*Binds and Barrels*? I love it."

"Me too," Adam agrees, nodding with approval.

Anthony rolls his eyes, his voice dripping with sarcasm. "Okay, let's be clear. You just stole my name and swapped in synonyms. But yeah, sure, let's pretend it's genius."

The room fills with laughter, and for the first time in my life I feel like I truly have my family.

CHAPTER TWENTY

Avery

After a week of nonstop visits to *Binds and Barrels*, I finally tell my siblings I need to shift my focus back to the Devils. With the charity event coming up on Saturday, everything has been planned and confirmed for weeks, but the golden rule of event planning is to expect chaos in the final days. Between juggling the details and putting out small fires, I've barely had a chance to see Chase all week.

On a brighter note, Campbell officially backed out of the bid, and after a few conversations between Abigail and his lawyer, the divorce papers were signed. Once the judge finalizes everything, I'll officially be a divorced woman. It's a strange feeling—one that hits me harder than I expect. While I'm relieved to close the chapter on our marriage, I've known Campbell my whole life. Despite the distance and coldness between us, I never imagined a future where he wasn't somehow part of it.

This morning, I'm having breakfast with the WAGs to review the speeches and awards for the upcoming charity event. Typically, this kind of recognition happens at the end-of-season banquet, but those are exclusive to the team and their families. This event, however, is for the entire community, and hearing the players get kudos from their loved ones before the season starts will add a special touch for everyone.

When I arrive at the restaurant, Jemmeye is already waiting near the front entrance, her smile warm and inviting. The sunlight catches on her dark curls, and she waves excitedly when she sees me.

"Hi!" I say, pulling her into a hug. The gesture feels both comforting and strange. Physical affection is still something I'm learning to embrace. The so-called friends I used to have were anything but affectionate, and my relationship with Campbell was a masterclass in distance. Now, being surrounded by people who show me they care in ways that align with my love language feels like a breath of fresh air, but it also leaves me a little unsteady.

With Chase, it's different. It came so naturally that I often don't even notice I've gone in for a kiss or I've been grazing his hand until it's already happened. But with friends, it's new territory: connection without conditions.

"Are we the first ones here?" I ask as we step inside the restaurant, the faint aroma of coffee and citrus wafting through the air.

"Yes," Jemmeye says, glancing at her phone. "But I just got a text from Tina and Ashley—they're almost here. And some of the newer women mentioned that they're on their way too."

"Great!" I say with a smile, sliding into my seat at the table already set with polished silverware, sparkling glasses, and pitchers of orange juice ready for mimosas. When I made the reservation a couple of weeks ago, I'd told the staff to prepare for a flexible headcount, unsure how many people would show up. But judging by Jemmeye's response, we'll easily fill this ten-person table.

As we wait, the nerves creep in, tightening my chest. I glance at Jemmeye, texting effortlessly, and then at the empty seats around us. These women are here for their husbands or boyfriends, their place in this world firmly established. I'm just someone helping with the logistics of their event, a little outside the circle. But still, I can't help but want them to like me.

Within fifteen minutes, our group has grown to fourteen, and the servers are amazing enough to pull up another table to accommodate.

"With the charity gala this weekend, I wanted to bring together all the significant others who signed up to do speeches for their guys. I also want to make sure none of you have lingering questions—or any other ideas I should consider for the event."

The table quiets for a moment, the hum of the restaurant filling the silence. Jemmeye, my number one cheerleader and ever-supportive friend, gives the table a quick scan, waiting to see who will speak up first. Her small smile and relaxed posture send the message: It's okay to jump in.

Finally, one of the newer WAGs, a petite blonde named Mia, leans forward with an eager expression. "I've never done anything like this before, and TJ and I just started dating a few months ago," she says. "Do you have tips on what we should say?"

And just like that, the ice begins to break. I smile, trying to put her at ease. "Honestly? Keep it short and sweet, and avoid saying anything that'll get him too embarrassed. Unless that's your goal, in which case, please carry on."

A few people laugh, and Mia giggles nervously. "Noted. No stories of the time he scaled my apartment building drunk and half-naked."

"Exactly," I say, nodding sagely. "But if you do have video evidence of this night, please send it to me. Purely for research purposes."

"Wait," Tina chimes in, holding up her mimosa like she's about to toast. "Are we allowed to roast them? Because I've been dying to bring up the time my husband tried to cut his own hair during quarantine and ended up with a reverse mullet."

"You mean just bangs?" Ashley gasps, nearly choking on her drink.

"Yes!" Tina exclaims. "Just bangs. I married a man who looked like a deranged boy band member for two weeks until he finally admitted defeat and shaved his head."

The entire table dissolves into laughter, even the servers glance over, grinning as they refill our pitchers.

"Maybe let's save roasts for a less public event. Honestly, my main goal for the event is just to show all the players a little love and appreciation before the season starts, and for me, a thank you to all of them for being such rock stars at these charity events."

"So, I have a question," Kimmy interjects with a sly, almost predatory grin, as she leans back and takes a slow, deliberate sip of her drink. Her eyes glint with mischief, and I can already sense where this is headed. "Who's handling Chase's speech?"

My throat tightens, and my pulse quickens. *Keep it together, Avery.* "His sisters are flying in. He mentioned it last week," I reply, striving for a neutral tone.

Kimmy's grin deepens as she leans forward. "He's not dating anyone?" Her tone is casual, but the pointed question feels anything but. Clearly, she's caught wind of the rumors about Chase and me—or maybe she spotted me in his jersey after the charity game.

My professional mask snaps into place, locking my emotions away. "Not that I'm aware of," I say, meeting her gaze evenly. "But having his sisters here adds a nice touch. There's a good mix of significant others, siblings, parents, and friends attending, which keeps things well-rounded. Any other questions?"

Jemmeye, sharp as ever, clocks the shift in my tone and jumps in to diffuse the tension. "So, ladies, what's everyone wearing?"

Her responses start a frenzy of chatter about floor-length vs. mid-thigh-length dresses, up-dos versus down-and-curled hair, and smoky eyes versus natural. As the conversation sweeps the table, I catch Jemmeye's eye and send her a silent thank-you. She smirks knowingly, and I grab my mimosa, draining nearly the entire glass in one gulp.

I'm so far in over my head, I might as well be drowning.

***

After nearly an hour and a half of listening to the endless chatter, I'm utterly overstimulated. My brain is fried, and the only thing keeping me upright is the thought of a hot bath and room service waiting back at the hotel. Only two more comments about Chase and me are tossed around—both from Kimmy, of course—but something about her tone has me on edge. It's like she knows something I don't.

I keep replaying the moments in my head as I stride through the lobby, past the concierge desk. Cedric catches my eye instantly.

"Avery," he calls out, his tone as steady as ever.

I groan, dragging my feet to a stop. "I don't have a check-out date yet, Cedric. Can we just plan for forever?"

"It's not that. Here," he says, handing me a large yellow envelope. "This came for you today."

The envelope feels heavier than it should. My eyes zero in on the sender's address, and my stomach plummets—Campbell's lawyer.

"Oh, great," I mutter, my fingers tightening around the edges.

"But no, we can't book you forever." Cedric presses, a faint smile softening his insistence. "We need a new date by next week. Please, Avery."

He emphasizes the word please, but his words barely register. My focus is glued to the envelope, my heart thudding in my chest like a warning drum.

"Avery?" Cedric repeats, pulling me back from the haze.

"Huh? Yes. Okay. I'll figure it out," I blurt, clutching the envelope tighter as I make my way to the elevators.

The doors close, sealing me into solitude, and I rip the envelope open with trembling hands. The neatly printed words confirm what I already knew but hadn't fully processed: my divorce is finalized.

A wave of exhaustion crashes over me, dragging me under. My nerves feel like live wires, sparking with a mix of relief, sadness, and something unnameable. This is my Achilles' heel—I've never learned how to handle my emotions. I only know how to keep moving forward, pretending nothing fazes me.

When the elevator dings, I step out into the quiet hallway. My feet feel like lead as I move toward my door, but then I see him—Chase. He's leaning casually against the wall, arms crossed, waiting for me.

I've never wanted to run toward and away from someone as much as I do now. My body is drawn to him like a magnet, aching for his comfort, while my mind screams to keep my distance.

"Chase." I sigh as I approach him.

"Hi, beautiful," he greets me with a soft smile, and just like that, warmth blooms low in my belly. "How was brunch with the ladies?"

"A lot," I admit with a nervous laugh, running a hand through my hair. "My nerves are shot, to be honest."

"Yeah, that's usually how I feel after those gatherings too." He chuckles. "Hey, guess what?"

"What?" I ask, leading us inside my room and collapsing onto the bed.

"My apartment will be ready in two weeks!" His grin is infectious. "I just got the call an hour ago."

"Chase, that's amazing!" I exclaim, a genuine smile breaking through the fog of my emotions. I spring up and throw my arms around him, hugging him tightly. I know he's been so excited about his apartment, and it's getting close, and seeing him be excited makes me happy.

I pull away from the hug and meet Chase's soft lips. The warmth spreads from my lips down to my toes. When Chase breaks the kiss, a huge smile stretches across his face. He brushes a strand of hair from my cheek and looks at me like I'm his whole universe.

"I love you, Avery," he says.

Four words. Just four words, and everything stops.

CHAPTER TWENTY-ONE

Chase

The words leave my mouth effortlessly, like a breath I've held for too long. The instant they're out, my entire body feels electrified, every nerve exposed. It's a high—until I see her reaction.

Avery freezes. Her hands, which had been loosely resting around my neck, have dropped to her sides. Her shoulders stiffen and her face drains of color.

"I—uh—I..." she stammers, her eyes darting anywhere but to mine. She looks like a deer in headlights, paralyzed and helpless.

The silence stretches out, heavy and oppressive, but I force myself to speak, to fill the void. "I know things are more complicated for you, Avery. I know that. But I didn't want you not to know how I feel about you."

I'm trying to sound calm and confident, like her response—or lack thereof—doesn't crush me. But I'm 100 percent unraveling. This has never happened to me before. I've never been this vulnerable with anyone, and been shut down so quickly.

She backs out of my hands, breaking what little connection we had left. "My divorce isn't even finalized yet, Chase."

"I know," I say quietly, trying to steady myself, even as she turns slightly away from me, putting more distance between us.

"Are you freaking out because you think this is too fast, or is it because you don't feel the same?" The question comes out sharper than I intend, the edge in my voice betraying the hurt I'm trying to bury.

She exhales shakily and rubs her temples like she's fighting off a migraine. "I don't even know how to answer that."

The words hit me like a gut punch. I want to be patient, to let her sort through whatever storm is raging inside her, but my chest tightens and my heart feels like it's splintering.

"I love you, Avery," I say again, softer this time, pleading. I see her flinch at my words, like a knife twisting in my chest. "I know that might scare you. And I'm sorry if it does. But I'm *not* sorry for how I feel."

Her gaze finally meets mine, and I see the conflict swimming in her eyes.

"I want more, Avery. I don't want to wait for some arbitrary amount of time to move forward with you. I want us. I want you."

She sighs, the sound full of exhaustion and something close to resignation. "Chase, please. Try to see this from my side. I'm barely divorced. We both live in a hotel, for God's sake. We're not even—"

"Dating?" I cut her off, shaking my head. "Those are just excuses, Avery. You're hiding. You're scared."

I can't stand still anymore. My legs move before I can stop them. Every step feels like I'm ripping myself away from her, but I can't keep standing here, begging for her to love me.

"I'm going to give you the space you need," I say, my voice tight with restraint. "But I won't do this halfway anymore."

For the first time, she stands up, a spark of energy in her movements. It's the most alive she's been since the moment I said *I love you.*

"And if I don't accept your ultimatum?" she challenges, her voice sharp.

I pause with my hand on the doorknob, turning to face her one last time. "It's not an ultimatum, Avery. But if we're not working toward the same end goal, then what's the point?"

Even with her staying silent, it takes everything in me not to turn back, to close the gap between us and take her in my arms, but I can't, not like this.

So I follow my brain and broken heart out the damn door.

***

After a full twenty-four hours of hiding out in my room—avoiding every hallway, elevator, and common space just to make sure I didn't run into Avery—I've officially reached a new low. I finally got hungry and bored, so I am now not only hiding from a girl, but running away back to my mommy.

I would be more embarrassed, but I can't possibly feel any worse than I already do. I wish this were just that my ego is bruised, but my ego has nothing to do with it. I'm crushed because I felt like we had this connection, this friendship and then this love and crazy attraction to each other on top of it, and my biggest fear was confirmed.

We just aren't on the same page.

After a long self-deprecating drive with lots of Adele and Noah Kahan blaring through the speakers, I find myself sitting at my childhood kitchen counter, nursing a cup of coffee that's gone cold, with my twin sisters sitting across from me, wearing matching expressions of disbelief.

"You told her you loved her, and she just froze, and then you gave her an ultimatum, but told her it wasn't an ultimatum and then just left?" Meghan says, dragging the last word out like it's physically painful for her to hear.

"Yep," I say. "That about sums up the shitshow of my life and this is why you both should never date," I say, narrowing my eyes at them.

Sara leans back, crossing her arms. "Well, duh. She's probably scared. You're Chase freaking Matthews. I'd be terrified too."

Meghan smacks her arm. "Don't encourage him. You're supposed to be the voice of reason here."

"Oh, please. He doesn't need a reason, Meg. He threw reason out the door back in the city. He needs a strategy," Sara counters, flipping her long braid over her shoulder like she's gearing up for battle.

I stare at them bewildered. "I don't need a *strategy*. I just need—" I stop mid-sentence, unsure of what I even want to say. "I don't know. I need her to trust me. I need her to make the first move and just trust us."

My sisters exchange a glance, the kind of twin telepathy that always makes me feel like I'm the third wheel in my own family. Then, in perfect unison, they shake their heads and say, "Men."

Meghan leans forward with her elbows on the counter. "What's the plan now? You gonna mope around here forever, or are you gonna win her back?"

I glare at her. "I'm not moping."

"Oh, you're definitely moping," Sara cuts in, pointing her spoon at me like a weapon. "And honestly? It's embarrassing for all of us. You're supposed to be the cool, charming one."

"It's fine, Chase. Your sisters will take care of it." Meghan's tone suddenly conspiratorial.

My eyebrows shoot up as a sinking feeling settles in my gut. "What the hell does that mean?"

Before I can get an answer, they hop off their stools, sharing a weirdly determined look that makes me even more suspicious.

"Don't worry about it," Meghan says breezily, waving me off as they head toward the stairs.

"Seriously, what does that mean?" I repeat, louder this time, but they ignore me, disappearing up the steps with matching smug smiles.

As I'm about to follow them and demand answers, my mom walks into the kitchen, holding a laundry basket. She looks up at me, then at the retreating backs of my sisters, and lets out a laugh.

"What's with them?" I ask, gesturing toward the stairs.

"They started watching the original *Gossip Girl* last week with some friends," she says, setting the basket on the counter. "It's making them a little...toxic."

I groan, sinking back into my seat. "Great. That's exactly what I need—teenagers binging an early aughts teen drama."

Mom chuckles and pats my shoulder, her touch warm and grounding. She sinks into the chair beside me, crossing her legs like she's settling in for a long talk. "Now talk to your mom," she says, her tone soft but insistent. "Are you okay, sweetheart?"

The knot in my chest tightens, and I stare at the mug in my hands, absently tracing the rim with my thumb. "I don't know, Mom," I admit quietly. "I'm just hurt. I don't know what I'm doing anymore, and I feel like an idiot."

Her expression softens as she leans forward, resting her elbows on her knees as she studies me. "Sometimes people aren't ready when you are, Chase. That doesn't mean it's over, it just means you have to decide if you're willing to wait."

I let out a long breath and lean back in my chair, staring at the ceiling like it holds the answers. "What if I'm waiting for something that'll never happen? What if I'm just setting myself up to get crushed?"

Mom reaches over, gently squeezing my hand. "Then at least you'll know you gave it your all. Love isn't always easy, Chase. I know you think love means big leaps and loud declarations, but it's also about being quiet and patient for that person."

I shake my head. "You and Dad made it look easy, you were always on the same page. How did you do it?"

Her laugh is soft, tinged with nostalgia. "Honey, your father and I were together for over five years before you came along. So yes, what you saw was a time in our relationship where we loved each other fiercely, but there were years when it wasn't loud—it was quiet, patient, and really hard. Times I wanted to run—when he came back from deployment he was different, and so was I. We had to relearn each other. And then there was the miscarriage before you came along."

I glance at her, startled. She rarely talks about the baby they lost.

She takes a deep breath, her eyes far away. "That was one of the hardest things we ever went through. We had to lean on each other in ways we didn't know how to at first. It wasn't about grand gestures or perfect moments—it was about showing up, even when it was hard. Especially when it was hard."

Her gaze locks onto mine, clear and steady. "Love grows in those quiet moments."

Her words hit me like a wave, the truth of them sinking deep into my chest. "So you're saying I should wait? Even if it means I could be waiting to just get screwed over?"

She smiles, tilting her head slightly. "I'm saying if you want someone to be loud with their love for you, you need to be willing to be quiet and steady for them."

I nod, her words settling over me. "Thanks, Mom," I say, my voice low but sincere.

CHAPTER TWENTY-TWO

Avery

I can't point out a single point in time when I've been as miserable as I am right now—and that's saying something, considering less than three months ago, my mother was alive, I was still married, and my life, while far from perfect, had a fragile but stable kind of order. Now, I'm living out of a suitcase in a suite too perfect for the mess I've become, and I've nearly read all my mother's journals, which have sent me on a completely different type of spiral.

Lying in bed, I can't focus on the comfort of the high-thread count sheets wrapping me like a cocoon or the floor-to-ceiling windows that offer a breathtaking view of the city skyline. None of it matters. All I see is the sweatshirt I threw off my body as soon as Chase walked out the door, that now lies in the middle of the floor, and plates of food I've ordered sitting untouched. Even the air feels heavy, like it's weighed down by everything I can't bring myself to face.

And it's all because of Chase.

Some guy I met, who came crashing into my life like a hurricane and told me he loved me. And I couldn't say it back.

The moment he said those words, everything inside me screamed to run to him, to throw my arms around him and tell him I wanted the same things he did. But instead, I froze. I watched the vulnerability in his eyes harden, and I let him walk away.

And now, the charity gala is two days away. The thought of being in the same room with him, pretending like everything is fine, feels like a sick form of torture.

I stare at my phone on the nightstand. I've drafted a dozen texts and deleted them all. What could I even say? *I'm sorry for freezing like a coward. I'm obsessed with you, but the idea of actually saying I love you makes me want to vomit.* I have a feeling that wouldn't go over too well either.

I close my eyes and take a deep breath, but it does nothing to calm me. The more I lie here, the worse it gets. Every second feels heavier than the last, suffocating me under the weight of everything I haven't said.

"Get up, Avery. Come on. Don't be this girl," I mutter as I finally swing my legs over the side of the bed, the cool hardwood floor grounding me briefly. My gaze catches on the sweatshirt again—Chase's sweatshirt—crumpled in the middle of the floor and the sight of it stirs a mix of regret and anger that propels me to move and get out of this room as quickly as possible.

I stumble into the bathroom, allowing the cold from the marble countertops to awaken my senses. I look in the mirror, hating the sight of the dark circles and puffy eyes from crying. I quickly apply some concealer and throw on a simple black dress, not wanting to bother with pants. Twenty minutes later, I'm in the backseat of a black town car, the Four Seasons fading into the distance behind me. The driver doesn't ask questions after I give him Abigail's work address and muttering something about needing to see my sister.

The city rushes past in a blur of lights and movement, but I barely notice. My thoughts are stuck on Chase, on how he looked at me, the sharp pain in his expression when I didn't respond, and how his voice sounded when he told me I needed to decide what I want.

I dig my nails into my palm, the sting keeping me from spiraling too far. When the car pulls up to her firm, I'm hit with a wave of nerves. The building is imposing, all sleek glass and steel, the kind of place that screams power and ambition. I hesitate for a moment, my hand hovering over the door handle.

What am I even doing here?

But before I can second-guess myself, the driver steps out, opening my door with a polite smile. I force my legs to move, stepping out of the car.

Inside, the lobby is just as intimidating as the exterior—polished floors, towering ceilings, and a receptionist with a smile so perfect it feels rehearsed. I give her

Abigail's name, and she points me toward the elevators without missing a beat.

The office is buzzing with quiet activity, associates moving with purpose, their faces lit by the glow of computer screens. Abigail's assistant, a polished woman with sharp eyes and an air of efficiency, greets me with a raised brow.

"Hi, I don't know if you remember me. I'm Avery, Abigail's sister," I tell her assistant I've seen the few times I've been here before.

"Do you have an appointment?" Her tone edges on the side of annoyance, but before I can respond, I see Abigail stepping out of her office, meeting my eyes almost immediately.

"Avery?" she says, her tone laced with concern as she strides over. "What are you doing here? Is everything okay?"

"Yeah, I'm okay. Do you have some time to talk?"

"Yes, of course. Come on, let's go into my office," she says as she starts leading the way into her office. "Kim, hold my calls until I'm done."

Kim nods in acknowledgement as the door slowly closes behind us.

"So, what's up? Is everything okay?" she asks, her tone soft as she guides me to the plush chair across from her desk.

The knot in my chest loosens slightly as I sink into the chair across from Abigail.

"I think I messed up," I blurt out, the words tumbling before I can stop them. "And I know we don't normally do this whole...talking thing, but I need someone, and you're who I thought of."

Abigail tilts her head, offering a small smile. She reaches across her desk, her hand finding mine in an uncharacteristically tender gesture for the two of us, and the contact almost makes me flinch. "I'm glad you came."

"Are you, though?" I reply, my voice dripping with sarcasm as I arch an eyebrow.

She squints at me like I just mispronounced a word she taught me. "I can be uncomfortable and still happy we're pushing through it."

"Who knew my sister could have such wise words?" I say, my voice teetering between sincere and teasing.

"Who knew mine was such a smartass?" she fires back without missing a beat.

We both laugh, the sound breaking some of the tension.

"So," she continues, sitting back in her chair, "what's going on? Is it the business or Campbell?"

"Chase," I admit, the name slipping out before I can stop myself.

Abigail's eyebrows shoot up as her lips twitch into a knowing grin. "Ah, the hot NHL player you're living with."

"I am *not* living with him." I scoff in disbelief.

"Fine," she concedes, rolling her eyes dramatically. "The hot NHL player who lives in the same hotel as you. By the way, we *should* discuss how much money you're wasting living there. But anyway—what did he do?"

I sigh, leaning back in the chair and covering my face with my hands for a moment before looking at her. "He told me he loves me."

Abigail freezes mid-smile, her expression mirroring mine from earlier.

"Yeah," I say, gesturing at her with both hands. "Imagine the way you just froze up but like ten times worse—and in front of said hot NHL player."

Her eyes widen, and she leans forward, resting her elbows on her desk. "So...what did you do?"

"Nothing. I panicked," I admit, groaning. "I stated the obvious—that we barely know each other, I'm still *legally* married, and that it's completely insane."

Abigail's lips twitch as she fights back a smirk. "Okay, but...do you love him?"

"How am I supposed to know?" I throw my arms up in frustration. "Like, seriously, I have *zero* idea what that word even means."

Abigail tilts her head, studying me. "You know, he didn't just call Anthony about the charity fair," she says, her voice softening. "He called all three of us. Chase cared enough to track down our numbers, tell us to come support you, and make sure you weren't standing there alone. Campbell never did that."

I stare at her, stunned. "He called you guys?"

She nods, her fingers tapping idly on her desk. "He did. And look, I don't claim to be an expert in love. At least you've been married—I'm flying blind here. But the way I saw you two looking at each other that day? That's how I imagine two people who are completely in love look. It's how I'd want someone to look at me."

Her words hit me harder than I expected, and I shake my head slowly. "I can't believe he did that."

Abigail leans back in her chair, tapping her fingers on the desk as she watches me. "Mom and Dad did a number on all of us, didn't they?" she asks, but I know it's a rhetorical question.

"We're all screwed up in one way or another—at this point, I just wish Mom left more than some journals explaining why we grew up the way she did."

Abigail tenses at the mention of the journals, her fingers stilling.

"Have you read any of them yet?" I ask cautiously.

She shakes her head quickly. "I'm glad you and Anthony are reading through them and that they led us to *Binds and Barrels*, but I don't need to read them."

I nod in understanding. I can't blame her—we all have our own ways of coping. And honestly, I don't know if I could tell her that the journals have brought me closure or just raised more questions.

"Have you finished them?" she asks after a moment.

"All but the last one," I admit, glancing down at my hands.

"The one from when she was pregnant with you?"

"Yep—and there are no more after that. At least not that I've found."

"Well," she says after a moment, "the good news is, you don't have to have all the answers right now. But maybe you should stop telling yourself what you *don't* know and start figuring out what you *do*."

I blink at her, caught off guard by the insight. "Who *are* you, and what did you do with my sister?"

"Shut up." She laughs, tossing a pen at me. "Now go figure it out, smartass."

I stand up, brushing my hands against my thighs, ready to leave. As I turn to the door, a thought strikes me, and I glance back. "I have my final charity event for the Devils this weekend. It's a black-tie gala at the MET. Interested in being my date?"

She raises an eyebrow, leaning back in her chair. "Is that guy who was annoying me at the fair going to be there—Billy Baker?"

I don't miss how her cheeks flush ever so slightly, and I smirk. "Why, yes, he is. Is that a problem, Ms. Abigail Keenan?"

She rolls her eyes and tosses another pen, which I dodge this time. "Get out of here—and text me the details."

I grin as I head toward the door, glancing over my shoulder. "I'll see you later."

***

Abigail's words linger in my mind as I step into my hotel room, their weight settling somewhere between my chest and my stomach.

Still riding the ripple of courage her words stirred in me, I pick up the phone and order three dirty martinis and a slice of cheesecake—because if I'm about to dive into my mother's final journal, I'll need both the liquid courage and the comfort food.

When the knock comes at the door, I tip the room service attendant generously, setting the tray on the small table by the window.

I sink into the plush mattress, propping myself up with pillows, the tray on my lap. The martini glass feels cool and heavy in my hand, and the first sip is crisp and bracing. Setting the glass aside, I reach for the worn journal on the nightstand—the last of my mother's words, the one I've been avoiding for weeks.

My fingers hesitate on the cover, tracing the soft edges where time and use have worn the material smooth. *Just open it,* I tell myself silently, taking a deep breath. With another sip of my martini, I flip open the journal and let the pages fall to where her story ended.

CHAPTER TWENTY-THREE

Avery

The sun creeps over the skyline, painting the city in soft hues of pink and gold. It's just past 6 a.m. and I'm still perched by the window, watching the world wake up while my mind refuses to rest. I've been staring at this view for hours, sleep slipping further out of reach with each passing minute.

Tonight is the charity gala—a night that should excite me, this is the final event for the New York Devils and a huge career milestone for me, but instead, dread coils tightly in my chest.

Sure, a little nervousness before a work event is normal, expected even. But this? This isn't the flutter of anticipation or the buzz of excitement. No, these are catastrophic tidal waves of anxiety and heartbreak, crashing over me in relentless, suffocating intervals.

There's still been no sight of Chase. After my talk with Abby, I mustered up enough courage to eat at the bar last night—equally terrified and hopeful that he'd be there too. But he wasn't. Now, knowing that the first time I'll see him since he walked out my door will be at a work event feels like it might actually kill me.

With a reluctant groan, I pull myself up to start my day. The gala doesn't begin until 5 p.m., but I'll be at the MET by 9 a.m., running on sheer determination and coffee. I make it in front of my mirror, taking in my appearance.

"It's game day, Avery. Get your shit together." I nod to myself and let my body and mind flip to work mode. There's too much to do—check on the decorators, confirm the caterers' arrival, oversee the delivery of gifts, and handle the inevitable last-minute disaster that always comes with events like this.

By the time I'm done, I'll barely have time to get make-up-ready, probably in some random hallway closet or bathroom, before slipping into my dress and hoping I look as composed as I'm pretending to be. I force myself into motion, grabbing a pair of leggings and a Devils shirt Chase left behind one night, before tying my hair into a loose bun.

I head to the kitchenette, flipping on the coffee maker and leaning against the counter as it gurgles to life. The faint aroma of caffeine offers a small comfort, but my stomach churns too much to enjoy it.

The gala is everything I've worked for these past few months—my final event for the New York Devils, a chance to prove myself on the biggest stage I've had, and I want this for my career and me. And yet, all I can think about is Chase. With a heavy sigh, I pour my coffee and take a long sip, letting the heat chase away some lingering tension.

By 7:30, I'm dressed and ready, my tote bag packed with my tablet, extra chargers, an emergency kit that includes everything from stain remover to duct tape, along with my dress and shoes, and I'm out the door.

The ride to the MET is quiet, and the city is just beginning to stir. My driver tries to converse politely, but my responses are clipped and distracted. My mind is already at the gala, running through the endless list of tasks awaiting me.

By the time I arrive, the decorators are already unloading their equipment. I check in with the event manager, who hands me a clipboard and rattles off the day's schedule. I nod, absorbing the information as I mentally map out the hours ahead.

The next few hours blur together in a whirlwind of logistics. I oversee the setup of the dining area, making sure every centerpiece is precisely as it should be. I double-check the caterers' arrival time, ensuring the hors d'oeuvres won't miss their cue. The gifts are delivered and carefully arranged in the reception area, each meticulously wrapped and tagged.

I'm in full work mode now, my anxiety replaced by a razor-sharp focus. But every so often, a flicker of panic sneaks in—Chase. Will he be there? How will he look at me? What will he say?

"Avery?" A voice pulls me from my thoughts, and I turn to see Tammy, my event assistant, tablet in hand and her usual calm demeanor intact.

"Yeah?" I ask, shaking off the momentary lapse.

"We've got a small issue," she says, breezy but pointed. "The ice sculpture's wrong. It's supposed to be a hockey stick and puck, but they delivered...whatever *this* is."

She gestures to the corner of the room, where a bizarre, semi-erotic, abstract block of ice sits, glistening under the light.

I blink, then let out a short laugh, the absurdity of it cutting through my nerves.

"Honestly, that's on me for thinking ice sculptures are a good idea," I mutter. "Okay, call the sculptor. If they can't fix it in time, we'll improvise. Flowers or something."

Tammy nods and heads off. I glance at the clock—just past 3:30 p.m. My window for getting ready is closing, and my nerves are creeping back in.

I exhale sharply, gripping my phone tighter. *Focus—one thing at a time.*

But no matter how hard I try to stay in the moment, one thought lingers in my mind: in just a couple of hours, I'll see Chase again. And I have no idea how to face him.

I grab my dress and heels, weaving through the bustling staff in the dining area. I say thank you to one of the florists fixing a centerpiece and step toward the cocktail section, my mind preoccupied with running through the checklist one last time.

The sound of the door opening makes me glance up.

And that's when I see him.

Time slows like a cruel joke as he steps into the room. He's wearing a navy suit that fits him *too* well, hugging his broad shoulders and tapering down to his lean waist.

His tie is perfectly knotted, and the crisp white shirt beneath the jacket contrasts against his warm tanned skin.
The way he walks—calm, confident, like he's entirely at
ease—sends a wave of heat rushing through me.

I freeze, clutching my dress and shoes tighter against
my chest as if they might shield me from the effect he's
having on me.

He moves with that quiet confidence he always has,
like he belongs wherever he is. He's scanning the room,
his sharp blue eyes taking in every detail, and for a moment I forget how to breathe. I stand there, rooted to
the spot, my heels digging into the polished floor as my
stomach twists in knots. He doesn't see me, and I should
be grateful for that, but instead my chest tightens with
something I can't quite name.

I can't let him see me—not like this. Not with my hair
in a messy bun, my makeup untouched, and my dress
hanging limp over my arm. Before my brain fully catches
up, my feet move, carrying me down the hallway toward
the nearest bathroom.

I push open the door and step inside, letting it close
softly behind me. My back presses against the cool wood
as I let out a shaky breath. My heart is pounding so loudly
it drowns out everything else.

Why does he have to look so good?

I glance at my reflection in the mirror and groan. My
cheeks are flushed, my hair is messy, and I look far from
composed. "Just get ready, Avery," I mutter, setting my
dress and shoes on the counter.

With a deep breath, I splash cold water on my face and try to refocus. There's no time to think about Chase or how good he looks or how my heart stuttered or stomach swarmed with butterflies when I saw him.

I grab my makeup bag, my hands shaking as I unzip it and pull what I need out, laying it on the counter. The fluorescent lights above cast a harsh glow on my reflection, and I take a steadying breath. *Get it together, Avery.* The gala won't wait for me to spiral.

Ten minutes later and my nerves are still buzzing, but as I add the finishing touches—deep eyeliner, a soft blush, and a swipe of neutral lipstick—I feel a little more like myself. Finally, I step back, smoothing the navy satin fabric of my dress against my hips. The gown hugs my figure in all the right places, the silky material catching the light as I move.

Just as I'm reaching for my heels, my phone buzzes on the counter, the screen lighting up with an unknown number. My first instinct is to ignore it, but tonight's event has too many moving pieces for me to take the risk. With a sigh, I pick it up.

"Hello?" I say cautiously.

"Hi!" two voices chirp in unison on the other end. "Is this Avery?"

I blink in surprise, straightening. "Yes. Who's this?"

"Oh, great!" one of them starts, their enthusiasm both endearing and overwhelming. "This is Sarah and Meghan—Chase's sisters. We were supposed to be at the gala tonight, but, uh..."

In the background, I hear the other one cough loudly, muttering something that sounds suspiciously like "flat tire."

"Yeah," the first voice continues, "a storm rolled in, and then, um, we got a flat tire. So, long story short, we're not going to make it."

My heart softens despite my nerves. "First of all, are you girls okay? Do you need someone to come get you?"

"Oh my god—no, we're totally fine!" the second voice interjects quickly. "The tow truck's here and our mom is on the way. We're good, promise. But we won't be there to give the toast tonight. Will someone else be able to cover for us?"

I pause—of course, the toast issue would be for Chase. "Uh... yeah, I'll figure it out. Don't worry about it."

"Okay, great! Thanks so much!" one of them gushes.

I glance at the time and realize I'm already cutting it close. "Listen, I should get out there, but I'll save your number. Call me if you need anything—and maybe give your brother a heads-up about tonight?"

"Totally!" they chime together. "Thanks, Avery! Bye!"

The line clicks off before I can respond, leaving me standing there in amused disbelief.

I take one last look in the mirror, smoothing my hair and running my hands down the silky navy fabric of my dress. I can't help but laugh at the irony of how perfectly it matches Chase's suit I'd seen him wearing earlier. The thought makes my stomach flip, but I shake it off quickly.

Now I have to figure out who is going to give the toast for Chase.

I step out of the bathroom, my heels clicking softly against the polished floor, the sound swallowed by the hum of activity in the hall. The gala is in full swing now, guests starting to trickle in, their laughter and chatter mingling with the soft strains of a string quartet echoing from the main room.

Finally taking a moment to take in the gala, I realize that the MET looks stunning—every detail is exactly as I'd envisioned. The centerpieces sparkle under the soft glow of the chandeliers, and the air is filled with the faint scent of lilies and champagne. I take a deep breath, letting the atmosphere wash over me.

Just one drink to steady your nerves and then it's show-time.

I weave through the clusters of early arrivals, exchanging polite smiles and nods as I make my way to the bar. My plan is simple: one glass of wine I'll nurse all night, just enough to take the edge off but not enough to distract me.

But then I see him. Chase.

He's standing near the bar, leaning casually against the counter, his tall frame impossible to miss. He's talking with Billy, Riley, Jamie, and Jemmeye. The navy suit looks even better now, fitting him like a second skin. His tie is slightly loosened, the top button of his crisp white shirt undone, giving him effortless charm. His hair is perfectly styled yet slightly tousled, and his whole presence makes my stomach swarm with butterflies.

Fuck. I love him.

I stop mid-step, my breath catching in my throat at my own thoughts. For a moment, I consider turning around, but my feet betray me, carrying me forward as if drawn to him by some magnetic force.

His gaze shifts, sensing my presence, and suddenly his eyes are on me. His expression changes instantly, his posture straightening, his lips parting slightly. The look on his face makes my heart race—a mixture of awe and desire.

He pushes off the bar, closing the distance between us in a few long strides.

I glance at Jemmeye, who sees me but doesn't move, just glances between Chase and me and gives a small, knowing smile.

Chase's eyes never leave mine, and I feel the heat rising to my cheeks as I try to keep my composure.

When he finally stops in front of me, his voice is soft but sure. "Avery," he says, his gaze sweeping over me, lingering on the navy satin of my dress before meeting my eyes again. "You look...incredible."

I want to jump him and slam my mouth against his. I feel my body exploding—desperate to touch him, but I force a small smile, clutching my phone tighter. "You look the same," I say, my voice steadier than I feel.

A grin tugs at the corner of his lips. "The same?" he teases. "Not even a little bit better? I mean, come on," he says, opening his suit jacket, giving me a little spin.

I roll my eyes, trying to hide the warmth spreading through me. "Fine. You look...superhot."

He chuckles, the sound low and familiar. His eyes soften, his gaze still holding mine as if he's trying to read every thought racing through my mind.

"Avery," he starts, his tone quieter now, more serious.

I clear my throat, cutting him off before he can say more. "I should...go say hi to everyone and then check on the caterers and servers," I mumble, stepping to the side, and hating myself for running.

But before I can slip past him, I feel his hand brush lightly against my arm, freezing me in place. The warmth of his touch surges through me, a sharp jolt that makes my pulse quicken. I glance up, our eyes locking. His gaze is intense as his lips curl into a small, hopeful smile. "Save me a dance later?"

I exhale a shaky breath, trying to steady the sudden rush of emotions coursing through me. I nod, my voice softer than I intend. "Yeah, of course."

I can't stand still for another second. My heart beats too loudly in my chest, and the knot in my stomach tightens with every passing moment. I practically run to Jemmeye, pulling her into a tight hug. "Hey, can we talk real quick?"

"Yes! Let's walk," she replies eagerly, a familiar spark of excitement lighting up her eyes.

I nod quickly and turn back to the guys, trying to force a casual smile. "Hi, guys, you all look amazing," I say, my voice slightly strained.

"You do too," James compliments with a playful grin just as Chase reenters the conversation, clapping his hand on James's shoulder with a brotherly affection.

"Abby is coming tonight," I add, addressing my comment to Billy, my voice tinged with teasing and curiosity.

"She is? Where is she?" Billy's eyes light up, scanning the crowd eagerly.

"Not yet." I laugh softly, shaking my head. "She texted me a little while ago. She'll be here closer to six."

I glance at Riley, wrapped up in a side conversation with Jemmeye. "I'm going to steal your girl for a minute," I say with a teasing grin.

Riley chuckles, pulling Jemmeye into his side as he kisses her slowly. "Come back soon." His voice is low and loving.

My chest tightens at the sight, and before I can fully process the feeling, I catch Chase's gaze, his eyes already on me. I quickly avert my eyes and gently tug Jemmeye's arm, guiding her toward the dining area. The noise of the cocktail hour is distant now, my focus narrowing to the steps before me. For the first time since seeing Chase, I finally manage to take a breath.

When we're far enough from the buzz of the crowd, I stop and turn to Jemmeye, running a hand through my hair in frustration. "Okay, I need your help. Chase's sisters got a flat tire and can't make it tonight, which means I need to find someone to give his toast. Do you think it's lame if one of the other guys does it?"

Jemmeye tilts her head to the side, a small, knowing smile playing on her lips. "Yes, that would be lame."

I groan, throwing my hands up in exasperation. "Ugh! Then who should do it? Toasts start in twenty-five minutes!" My voice wavers, the time crunch pressing down on me.

Her smile widens slightly, and she gives me that look, the one that says she's about to make a point I already know is true. "Avery, you already know who's perfect for this toast."

I shake my head immediately. "Jemm, I can't."

"Who else is going to do it? You're really going to let Chase be the only player who doesn't get a toast?"

"I—" My throat feels tight, and I swallow hard, forcing back the sting of tears threatening to spill. "Okay." My voice is quiet, resigned. "Let's just do this."

I'm so sick of frickin' speeches.

CHAPTER TWENTY-FOUR

Chase

My eyes dart around the room searching for her, drawn like a moth to a flame. Avery. She looked like a goddamn goddess the moment she walked in. That dress—sleek, dark, and hugging her curves like it was made for her—combined with the way her hair is swept to one side, exposing the delicate line of her neck. It made me want to drop to my knees right then and there.

When she stepped into the room, my instincts took over. I practically sprinted to her, and it took every ounce of willpower not to pull her into my arms and kiss her in front of everyone.

Now I'm trying to focus on anything but her, pretending to care about the stage, the auction, the chatter around me. But my patience is wearing thin. Before it completely dissolves, Avery steps onto the stage. My breath catches when she takes the mic in her hand, her lips parting in a confident smile. She's radiant, commanding the room with nothing more than her presence. My chest tightens as I watch her, equal parts awestruck and outright desperate to be near her.

"Good evening, everyone, and welcome to the New York Devils' annual charity gala," she begins, her voice clear and vibrant, carrying over the crowd. "This is the final event in our preseason charity series, and before we dive into toasts and speeches I want to thank each and every one of you for making this possible."

She pauses, her eyes scanning the crowd, the glow of the stage lights catching the glint of her earrings and the soft sheen of her dress. She pulls her phone from a pocket, glancing at it briefly before continuing.

"I promise to keep this short, but I'd love to share a few highlights from our earlier events. Our first preseason event was the Annual Youth Hockey Clinic—something that's become a pillar of the Devils' community outreach. This year, with the addition of a post-clinic charity game, we raised an incredible two hundred fifty thousand fifty thousand for underserved schools in the New York City area. Plus, we were able to donate fifty thousand to refurbish the kids' rink in the Bronx."

The crowd murmurs their approval, and I find myself leaning closer, my drink forgotten in my hand as I watch her light up the stage.

"The second event," she continues, her smile widening, "was the fan-favorite tailgate. We can all agree it's something we weren't entirely sure we could pull off—right, Neil?" She gestures toward Neil, who grins and gives a playful nod, eliciting laughter from the crowd.

"This event was my baby," Avery says, pride evident in her tone. "And I'm thrilled to share that between ticket sales, memorabilia auctions, and generous donations, we raised another two hundred thousand for the New York Kids for Kids Foundation. These funds will support families and children facing significant medical challenges."

She pauses, her eyes sparkling with excitement as she spins on stage, the crowd's energy rising with her enthusiasm.

"And now, this gala—our grand finale," she says, her voice lifting. "Yes, we've held galas before, but this year is special. We've introduced a silent auction with all proceeds being split between two incredible causes: the New York Women's Shelter and the New York Autism Center. If you haven't had a chance to place your bids yet, you'll find the items displayed in the back. Trust me, this is a cause worth supporting and the auction items are incredible."

The applause is instantaneous, a wave of approval filling the room. Avery's smile softens as she clasps her hands together.

"Of course, none of this would be possible without our incredible players—the heart and soul of this organization. So, before Neil and Coach take the stage, we'd like to celebrate the team in a more personal way. Tonight, we've invited some loved ones to offer special toasts to the players. To kick us off, I'd like to welcome a good friend of mine, Jemmeye, to share a toast for our captain, Riley."

The room erupts into applause as Jemmeye approaches the stage, but I barely notice. My eyes remain fixed on Avery as she steps to the side, her gaze scanning the crowd. For a moment, her eyes find mine, and the way she smiles and her eyes light up has my adrenaline in overdrive. She quickly turns back to the stage, refocusing her attention, and I force myself to do the same, shifting my focus to Jemmeye's toast—or roast, more like it. Laughter ripples through the crowd as Jemmeye pokes fun at Riley, but my mind drifts.

Billy's brother, whom he practically raised, flew in from Ohio to surprise him which was incredible to witness. Jamie and Riley's mom takes the mic next, her voice warm and proud as she shares stories that have everyone smiling.

Then it's my turn—or so I thought.

I glance around, scanning the room for my sisters. Where the hell are they? Pulling out my phone, I spot a text from Sara, timestamped twenty minutes ago.

> **Sara:** You'll thank us later. Have a good night. XOXO.

What the hell does that mean?

Before I can make sense of it, Avery's voice echoes through the speakers, and my eyes snap to the stage. She's standing there again, microphone in hand, making small, deliberate steps back and forth, pacing like I've seen her do a hundred times in her hotel room. I always teased her for it, but seeing her doing it here makes my chest tighten.

"So, originally Chase's sisters were supposed to give a toast," she begins, her voice steady but with a nervous edge I recognize instantly. "But, uh, they're presumably having some car trouble, so, Chase..." She glances at me, her cheeks flushed a deep pink even under the stage lights. "I hope it's okay that I'm stepping in."

Her eyes meet mine for a brief second, and I see her take a deep breath before continuing.

"I met Chase...umm...after a few big life changes," she says, her voice soft but clear. "And somehow, a complete stranger I ran into at the front desk of a hotel became a lifeline and a support system I can't imagine living without."

I inhale sharply, her words hitting me square in the chest. The room fades, and all I can see is her, like a montage in my mind—flashes of the night she checked into the hotel, the endless hours of *two truths and a lie,* the way she looked when she showed up at my door to stay the night, the carnival.

"I've never met someone who knows exactly what they want and goes for it with the kind of clarity and confidence Chase does," she continues, her voice trembling slightly. "He's fearless and loyal, and brings light into every moment he's in. It's...it's why it was so easy to fall in love with him."

My heart stops.

"And," she adds, her voice dipping, "why it's so scary to think about losing him."

Did she just say she's in love with me?

"So, Chase"—she raises a champagne glass in the air—"here's to you and the amazing season I know you have ahead of you. I love you."

I don't even realize I'm gripping the edge of the cocktail table until my knuckles ache. All I know is that I want—no, *need*—to get to her. Within seconds, I'm on the stage, my hands cupping her face. Her eyes glisten with unshed tears, but she's laughing softly, a sound that cracks open something in my chest.

The mic in her hand falls limply to her side, and she whispers loud enough for only me to hear. "Does this mean you're not done?"

"Oh, baby," I murmur, my thumbs brushing her cheeks. "I wasn't going anywhere. You could've taken all the time in the world, and I'd still be here when you were ready."

Her breath catches, a quiet sob slipping free as I lean in and capture her lips with mine.

The room erupts in cheers and applause, but it all fades into background noise. All I can feel is her—soft, warm, and all mine.

She laughs against my lips, and I can't help but laugh with her, the sound muffled between us. My body feels electrified, like every nerve is alive and buzzing. Reluctantly, because I know we are standing in front of easily a few hundred people, I pull away.

Her cheeks are flushed, her smile radiant as she looks up at me. "I love you, Chase Matthews," she says, her voice unwavering.

"And I love you, Avery Keenan," I reply, my voice steady and sure. "It's you and me now."

She nods, her grin stretching ear to ear, and then, to my amazement, she lifts the mic back to her mouth.

"Well," she starts, her voice ringing through the speakers, "sorry about that *very* unprofessional display, but I mean—come on!"

The crowd roars with laughter, and she waves playfully at them.

"Anyway," she continues, clearing her throat as if to reset the mood, though her cheeks are still glowing. "Next up is Seth Tibs to give a toast for our second-year defenseman, Tim Tibs."

Seth climbs the stage, grabbing the mic from Avery with a wide grin. "Well, that's gonna be a tough act to follow," he jokes, his voice full of humor.

Avery and I exchange a glance, both of us grinning like fools, and without a word we step off the stage together. I practically haul her out of the area and into a makeshift coat closet near the bar. The moment we're behind the curtains, away from the glaring lights and hundreds of eyes, I pull her into my arms again, holding her tightly against me.

"Bold move, mystery girl," I murmur, guiding her backward until the table's edge presses against her.

Her hands splay against my chest, as she looks up at me with wide, earnest eyes. "I meant every word, Chase. I was scared. Feelings are hard for me, and I let them get the better of me. I shouldn't have let you walk away."

We keep moving, slow and steady, until her back is against the wall. My hands slide up from her hips, tracing the line of her body until they cover hers, still resting on my chest.

"I shouldn't have walked out," I admit, my voice low and rough. "I was hurt, yeah, but I knew the pressure you were under—Campbell, your family, all of it. I shouldn't have pushed you so hard and then bailed when I didn't get the answer I wanted. I'm sorry, Avs."

"Don't be," she whispers, her voice steady and sure. "I needed that push. You make me feel things I've never felt before, Chase. You push me to be better, to be braver. And I love you for that. I love you so much."

The words hit me like a freight train, even though I heard her say them moments ago, but this—just the two of us, alone in the quiet—feels more real.

"Say it again," I demand, my gaze locked on hers.

Her lips curve into a soft smile, and she takes a tiny step closer, her voice steady and clear as she says, "Chase Matthews, I love you."

"I love you," I breathe as I close the last sliver of space between us, capturing her lips with mine. It's not hurried or frantic—it's deep and steady, as if I'm trying to memorize every part of this moment. My hands slide down the smooth fabric of her dress, resting at her waist as if to anchor her to me.

Her fingers curl into the fabric of my shirt, pulling me even closer. The way her body melts into mine is intoxicating, every barrier we've ever had fading into nothing. She tastes like everything I didn't know I needed.

"I love you," I whisper again against her lips, as if saying it once could never fully convey how much she means to me.

"Want to show me how much?" she teases, her sly grin lighting a fire in my chest.

I tuck a loose strand of hair behind her ear, my thumb grazing the soft curve of her cheek. "What exactly do you have in mind?"

She lets out a soft laugh, her forehead pressing against mine, her hand finding my hard dick straining against my tux pants.

I grin, my hands tightening on her waist, pulling her closer. "At your work event?"

Her smile grows mischievous. "Might as well make it a tradition," she whispers, her eyes gleaming with playful confidence.

I can't help but laugh. "Your wish is my command, darling."

CHAPTER TWENTY-FIVE

Avery

The coat closet sex-scapade leaves me feeling like my heart might actually burst. My dress is a little wrinkled and my hair feels slightly out of place, but Chase looks even more disheveled—not that he seems to care. He's tugging his jacket back into place, still wearing that smug, boyish grin that makes my stomach flutter.

I try smoothing the fabric of my dress, but my hands are shaking slightly. His grin hasn't wavered, and every time I glance at him, I can feel the heat creeping up my neck.

"You have to stop smiling like that," I whisper, attempting to sound stern but failing miserably. "If you walk out there looking like *that*, everyone will know what just happened—and I'll *definitely* lose my job."

He laughs, low and rich, his voice sending a fresh wave of warmth through me. "Not a chance. This is my face now. Permanent." He leans in, brushing a quick kiss across my lips, his breath warm and teasing. "You'd better get used to it, beautiful."

I huff, pretending to be annoyed, but the truth is, I don't want him to stop smiling—not now, not ever. "You're impossible," I mutter, pushing against his chest playfully before stepping out of the closet ahead of him.

The hallway feels colder than the small, intimate space we just left. My cheeks are still flushed, my lips feel swollen, and I'm positive my carefully applied makeup has taken a hit.

Chase stays close behind me, his fingers brushing the small of my back, guiding me forward. "Relax," he whispers, his breath grazing my ear. "You look stunning, and no one knows a thing."

I shoot him a look over my shoulder. "You don't know that."

He smirks, tilting his head toward the room. "Trust me. You're a goddess."

We step back into the dining area, and I immediately spot Neil standing near the bar with a glass of scotch in hand. The room hums with energy as guests mingle and laugh, the earlier speeches apparently over. A slight pang of guilt hits me for missing them, but then Chase's hand brushes mine, and that guilt dissolves into a quiet hum of contentment.

Neil's sharp gaze locks onto me, and he starts weaving through the crowd toward us.

"Avery!" he calls, his tone warm but authoritative. "I've been looking for you all night."

"Neil, Hi," I say nervously. "I'm sorry about earlier, I know that wasn't professional and it was not my intention to make a scene."

Neil waves me off, a lighthearted chuckle escaping him as he shakes his head. "Relax, Avery. You're too good for this knucklehead anyway." He gestures to Chase, who stands beside me, trying and failing to suppress a smug grin.

Chase lets out a mock-offended laugh. "I'm standing right here, Neil."

Neil smirks before turning his attention fully back to me. "But," he continues, his tone softening, "if you're happy with him, then more power to you. What I wanted to talk about has nothing to do with him. It's about you."

My stomach flips and I nod, encouraging him to go on, though my palms are starting to sweat.

"The team has been talking about this for a while now, and after tonight's event, I'm convinced. The Devils need a more permanent event director—someone who can bring in the kind of energy and turnout we have tonight. And after seeing what you pulled off with this preseason charity gala, it's clear you're the perfect fit. We'd be lucky to have you on the team on a more permanent basis."

My breath catches, this was the last thing I was expecting, but a permanent position with the New York Devils would be incredible if I could swing both the team events and *Binds and Barrels*.

"Wow, Neil," I manage, my voice barely above a whisper. "I'm—thank you. I'm honored."

"You've earned it, Avery," Neil says, clapping Chase on the shoulder as he leaves. "You're a natural. Think it over, and we'll talk the specifics on Monday."

Chase's hand brushes mine, grounding me as I look at him. "I told you that you were a goddess," he says, his voice filled with pride.

I let out a nervous laugh, shaking my head. "This is...I don't even know what to say. How do you feel about it? Working together more permanently, I mean?"

His expression softens, and he steps closer, the crowd and noise of the gala fading into the background. His voice drops, intimate and sure. "Baby, I'd be ecstatic to spend any extra time I can with you. But this isn't about me. This is about *you*—what you want, what makes you happy. I support you fully, no matter what you decide."

Déjà vu washes over me, taking me back to the moment months ago when I first got this job. Back then, I couldn't have fathomed how much having someone like him in my corner—someone who cares so deeply about my happiness and loves me boldly and unapologetically every single day—would transform me. The way Chase loves me has made me grow and become a better person. I don't want to be scared of love because I've never seen it. I can be my own example of love and family, with Chase and my siblings.

My hand tightens around his as I look up at him, ready to tell him just how much he means to me, when a burst of laughter pulls me out of focus. The noise draws our attention toward the bar at the far end of the gala hall.

There, leaning casually against the counter with a drink in hand, is Billy, grinning ear to ear, while Abigail stands next to him, her laughter ringing out like a melody. Chase follows my gaze and smirks.

"Looks like Billy's making some serious progress," he teases, his thumb brushing against mine in that familiar, comforting way.

"Not a chance," I reply with a laugh, shaking my head.

Chase quirks an eyebrow at me, clearly amused. "Care to make another bet?"

"Come on," I say, tugging his hand as we walk toward them. "Let's go investigate."

"Investigate?" he echoes, his laughter bubbling up.

"Yes," I say with mock seriousness. "If my sister has a crush, I need to know."

"Whatever you say," Chase says with a smirk, trailing behind me as we make our way to the bar.

"Well, hello, you two," I say brightly as we arrive. My eyes flick between Abigail and Billy, catching the subtle, telling glances they exchange. Meanwhile, Chase gives Billy a knowing look that practically screams *I see you, man*.

"Nice speech, Avery," Abigail quips, a smug grin on her face. "I'll admit it was better than your last one."

"Why did I invite you again?" I shoot back sarcastically, narrowing my eyes at her playfully.

"I don't know," she says, shrugging dramatically. "Considering I've barely seen you all night, it's a mystery."

"Well, I'm here now," I say, crossing my arms, feigning offense.

"Actually," Abigail starts, exchanging a glance with Billy, "we were just about to head out and grab some food. Do you guys want to come?"

"You're ditching already?" I pout, though the corners of my lips tug upward.

"Yeah," she says matter-of-factly. "Things are winding down, and all the auction winners get notified by email anyway. So—"

"Fine." I sigh, cutting her off. "I have to stay a bit longer, but call me tomorrow, please?"

"Of course," Abigail says, pulling me in for a hug. As we embrace, she leans closer and whispers, "Thank you" so softly I almost don't hear it.

I pull back, meeting her eyes, and smile. Maybe Chase was right—there's something there.

"Enjoy your late-night snack," Chase says, giving Billy a light clap on the back.

"Yeah, yeah," Billy says with a grin, his hand resting lightly on Abigail's back as they turn to leave.

As they walk away, I lean closer to Chase. "Okay, maybe she *does* like him," I admit.

He chuckles, wrapping an arm around my waist. "Told you. My boy's got charm."

I glance up at him, smirking. "Not as much as you, obviously."

"Obviously," he replies with mock arrogance, pulling me closer as we head back toward the main event.

***

After a few more hours of socializing, Chase and I are finally headed back to our hotel together. The energy of the gala still hums faintly in the air, but all I can think about is the man walking beside me. It's funny how much can change in a single day—how this morning I couldn't muster the courage to get out of bed and face him, and now I can't wait to get back into bed with him.

The crisp night air wraps around us as we step outside the car, the city lights casting a soft glow over his sharp features. Chase's hand finds mine, his thumb gently brushing over my knuckles as we walk in a comforting silence.

"What's going on in that beautiful head of yours?" he asks when we finally make it to the elevators.

I give him a soft smile, trying to play it coy. "How do you know I'm thinking? What if I'm just blissfully drunk and walking with you?"

Chase laughs, the sound low and warm, shaking his head. "I know you, Avs. The way your face crinkles when you're frustrated. The way you bite your bottom lip when you're focused. Or how you give yourself little pep talks before you do anything and think no one notices." His voice softens, his eyes holding mine like he's afraid I'll look away. "I notice. I notice everything when it comes to you. I call you mystery girl, but I know you, Avery Keenan."

My heart skips a beat—no, it's running wild, like it's trying to break free from my chest at his confession. Vulnerability isn't something I've ever been good at, but instead of running from it like I usually do, I lean into it.

"This morning," I start, my voice quieter now, "I had no idea how I would face you. I thought...I thought I ruined everything." I lift our clasped hands, a small smile tugging at the corner of my lips. "And now—" I take a deep breath, the honesty pouring out before I can stop it. "I'm still nervous, Chase. I could still screw this up. I've never been good at this kind of thing."

He stops walking, turning me toward him in the empty hallway. His free hand cups my face, his thumb brushing against my cheek. "Avery," he says firmly, but his tone is so gentle it feels like a balm to my anxieties. "We're both going to screw up. That's part of it. We're human, we just need to promise to figure it out together. We're a team."

"We're a team." I nod, my voice steady despite the emotions bubbling up inside me.

"Good," he says, his smile softening into something more intimate, more sincere. Then he lets out a small laugh, like he's remembering something funny.

"What?" I ask, my curiosity piqued.

"Well..." He scratches the back of his neck, looking a little sheepish. "I wasn't going to bring it up tonight, but there's something you should know about my sisters."

I raise an eyebrow. "What about them?"

"The flat tire," he says, grinning now. "They lied. They faked the whole thing."

"What?" I blink, processing his words.

"They know about us, and I think they thought they'd force your hand. I don't necessarily understand all of it, but they've been watching *Gossip Girl* and my mom says it's been making them a smidge toxic."

I snort, covering my mouth to stifle the laugh. "Frickin' Chuck Bass strikes again."

"What?" he asks, his grin growing as he watches me dissolve into laughter.

"Nothing. I respect the scheme, honestly, and it worked out in our favor, so cheers to *Gossip Girl*." I laugh.

Chase chuckles, leaning down to kiss my forehead, his lips lingering there before pulling back. "My new favorite show. I owe them one."

"You know...we will have to get them back somehow," I half-joke.

"Oh, absolutely," he says, his voice teasing as his hands slide to my waist. "Now, let's get to our room so that I can tear that beautiful dress right off your body."

I laugh, everything melting away and being replaced by pure desire. "Yes, please."

EPILOGUE

Avery

Three months later

It's the opening night of *Binds and Barrels,* and it feels like stepping into a dream. The past three months have been an absolute whirlwind, but tonight, as I take it all in, I know it was worth every sleepless night, every anxious moment.

The store is exactly how my mom described it in her journals, but it's also much more. It's the *four of us*. Every corner, every detail reflects each of us. Floral arrangements spill across the bookshelves, filling the air with the soft fragrance of peonies and gardenias—Abigail's touch. A section near the back is dedicated to vintage medical and law books—Adam's non-negotiable contribution, complete with a glass display case for the rarest finds.

Then there's the bar—a stunning centerpiece with live-edge countertops I tracked down from an Amish family in Michigan. Chase teased me relentlessly about the lengths I went to for these slabs of wood, even joining me on a weekend road trip to see them in person. But now, as they sit perfectly in place, their warmth and natural lines grounding the entire aesthetic, I know it was worth every mile and every joke at my expense.

At exactly 5 p.m., the bar officially opens, along with the cozy cigar lounge tucked away in the basement. The signature drink menu, a labor of love painstakingly crafted by Adam and our bartenders, feels like a tribute to both of us. It features two variations of Old Fashioneds—because Adam is unapologetically particular—a spicy margarita for me, and the crown jewel—The Cinzia Martini. A dirty martini with three olives, it's a small but meaningful nod to our mom's legacy.

The truth is, bringing my mom's dream to life hasn't erased the pain of the past or magically healed the wounds all four of us carry. I thought maybe it would. I hoped it would. And I still hope that one day it might. But what it *has* done is reconnect me with my siblings, and that's all I need.

We're a team now. We meet weekly for business, but it's so much more than that. We go to Anthony's fights together, cheering loudly from the front row. They've even come to some of Chase's games with me—well, Abigail hasn't missed a single one, but I suspect that has more to do with Billy than connecting with her siblings.

Tonight, everything feels in place. The store is packed with people—friends, family, and curious strangers drawn in by the buzz we've built. Abigail flits around the room like a social butterfly, chatting up every guest.

Adam is stationed near the vintage book section, talking animatedly with a professor from Columbia about rare medical texts. Anthony, towering and broad-shouldered, is by the bar, laughing with a group of his friends who came to support us.

And then there's Chase.

I spot him as the door opens, his tall frame backlit by the warm glow of the streetlights. He steps inside, looking effortlessly handsome in khakis and a thick navy sweater, a bouquet of white lilies in one hand and a mischievous grin on his face. My heart does its now-familiar flip at the sight of him.

He weaves through the crowd with ease, nodding and smiling at people who recognize him as the Devils' star forward. When he reaches me, he hands me the flowers and leans in, pressing a soft kiss to my temple.

"For you, mystery girl," he murmurs.

I smile, inhaling the sweet scent of the lilies. "You're late," I tease, but there's no real bite in my voice.

"Had to get something set up for after this," he says, slipping an arm around my waist. "Any chance you'll come somewhere with me after closing?"

I look up at him. "Any hints where?"

He leans down, brushing his lips against mine. "Nope. You just need to wait."

And together we turn to the crowd, hand in hand, ready to celebrate this fantastic night.

***

After a few hours, Abigail and Adam agree they'll close up, letting Chase sweep me away to his surprise. After a ten-minute drive, we arrive at his apartment building.

"You know, Chase, I love you, but you've been back here for a couple of months now, and I've been over plenty of times," I tease, giving him a playful nudge.

The past two months have been a blur of nights between his place and the Four Seasons, where I'm still technically living. I promised Cedric I'd give him a final move-out date by the end of the month—but I've said that before.

"Just follow me, smartass," he teases back, lacing his fingers through mine and tugging me toward the elevator.

As soon as the doors slide shut, I reach for him, my lips finding his instantly. That same electric current surges through me, the one I've felt since we first kissed. I never imagined I'd get this kind of love—passionate, patient, unwavering. It's everything I lacked growing up, everything I thought I had with Campbell but never truly did. Now that I have it, I can't fathom how I ever lived without it.

By the time the elevator doors open, I'm breathless, smiling as I step into his apartment. I remember the day we stood in this space, choosing designs before we were even an "us." I tease him all the time that he went with everything I liked, and he just grins—like he knew, even then, that we'd end up here together.

Chase slows his steps as we move through the entrance and into the kitchen. And that's when I see it.

White lilies—like the ones he brought to the store earlier—fill the room, their delicate petals softening the modern space. And on the counter, in bold, unmistakable letters, sits a sign:

Move in with me.

My breath catches. Tears prick at my eyes as I turn to him, my heart hammering.

"You want me to move in?" I whisper.

His hands frame my face, his eyes filled with so much love it makes my knees weak. "Baby, I want everything with you. I want to live with you. I want to marry you. I want to build a family and grow old with you. I want it all. But right now, this is me asking—begging, really—move in with me? Since the renovation, this has always been our place. I would've asked the second it was finished, but I didn't want to rush you. But I can't wait any longer. I want this to be ours—officially."

A laugh bursts from me, even as tears slip down my cheeks. My heart feels too full, like it might burst with happiness.

"It's about damn time."

Chase sweeps me off my feet, spinning me around as we laugh, tears mixing with joy. When he finally sets me down, his lips find mine again, a promise in every kiss.

I pull back just enough to grin at him. "But what will we do without the Four Seasons' drinks and steak?"

He chuckles. "That's easy. Weekly date nights. We can't let Cedric miss us too much."

I laugh, wrapping my arms around his neck as he kisses me again.

"I love you, Avery Keenan."
"And I love you, Chase Matthews."

ALSO BY

MARINA ALEXA

Check out my Amazon author page:
https://www.amazon.com/author/marinaalexa

Sign up for my newsletter and get updates first:
https://www.marinaalexa.com/

Follow me on social media:
Instagram:
https://www.instagram.com/authormarinaalexa
Threads:
https://www.threads.com/@authormarinaalexa
TikTok:
https://www.tiktok.com/@marinaalexaa
Pinterest:
https://www.pinterest.com/marinaalexab/

Made in United States
Cleveland, OH
24 November 2025

26575412R00144